Cooking for Harry

KAY-MARIE JAMES

Cooking for Harry

A LOW-CARBOHYDRATE NOVEL

Shaye Areheart Books
NEW YORK

Published by Shaye Areheart Books, New York, New York.
Member of the Crown Publishing Group, a division of
Random House, Inc.
www.randomhouse.com

SHAYE AREHEART BOOKS and colophon are trademarks
of Random House, Inc.

Printed in the United States of America

Design by Lynne Amft

Library of Congress Cataloging-in-Publication Data
James, Kay-Marie.
Cooking for Harry : a low-carbohydrate novel / Kay-Marie James.—
1st ed.
    1. Overweight men—Fiction. 2. Reducing diets—Fiction.
3. Married people—Fiction. 4. Weight loss—Fiction.
5. Cookery—Fiction. 6. Cooks—Fiction. I. Title.
PS3610.A445C66 2003
813'.6—dc22
                                         2003059590

ISBN 1-4000-4502-9

10   9   8   7   6   5   4   3   2   1

First Edition

For A-K P N

We'd sip tea with lemon
and sugar, share a red bowl
of popcorn and I'd be grateful
for it all: our family's pain
and sweetness, that love survived
these seasons and forgiveness
eased us into second chances.
—EDWIN ROMOND

CONTENTS

Cooking for Harry

In the Beginning

The bathroom scale was only one of many household appliances that hadn't survived our children. When you've got four—Amber and the twins came ten months apart, six years ahead of Jason—there are bound to be casualties, and when the value of one of those casualties falls anywhere below three digits, you consider yourself a soldier of good fortune. You thank God for letting Amber and the twins break the scale instead of, say, the washing machine. And the following year, when they actually *do* break the washing machine, you thank God that they are not yet old enough to wreck the car. And when you get the midnight phone call that begins, "Mom, we're fine, okay? Everything's fine, but we had a little accident . . . ," you thank God because, despite their best efforts, they have yet to burn the house down, a failure that you truly believe can be attributed only to Divine Intervention.

"Mary was a mother, too," Harry intones at every crisis. He went to Catholic school, served as a bashful altar boy—the whole nine yards. He'd even been making plans to enter Pittsburgh Seminary, much to his mother's delight. Then, at twenty, he discovered sex, by which I mean he discovered me. Needless to say, Mathilde Kligler was significantly less delighted about that.

"Jesus, Mary, and Joseph, pray for us," I reply. I'm the unlikely offspring of a lapsed Baptist mother and a Jewish father, but I've picked up a few things over the years that my grandparents on my mother's side—God rest their souls—would have called *Papist*. I know that St. Anthony is the patron saint of lost objects. I know that *mea culpa* means *sorry*. Mathilde Kligler never recovered from her only son's marriage to an infidel, but in my opinion, religious differences just don't matter that much. What matters is that two people see eye to eye on something equally spiritual, something that gives their lives direction, something—yes, I'll say it—*sacred* to them both.

For Harry and me, this particular something happened to be sex. Now and again, it still is. But, for the most part, what kept us happily in step with each other, aside from the children, was Harry's cooking. Or rather, Harry's cooking and our shared passion for eating. And I don't mean burgers and hot dogs and fries, though heaven help us, we'd eat those, too, if there was nothing else around. What I'm talking about is the sort of food my mother always called *too much fuss:* bisques and brioches, soufflés and saffron risottos and homemade ragus. It was nothing for Harry to whip up a little crème anglaise for an evening snack, dribble it over pears poached in wine. He candied his own ginger, blanched his own almonds. He braised, he sautéed, he caramelized. And me? I was his acolyte, his adoring altar girl. I passed the holy instruments. I scrubbed coq au vin off the golden pots.

Harry's kitchen career was born around the same time as the twins. It began with a simple indulgence, a secret treat: bowls of buttery popcorn after the last bedtime story had been read and the last lullaby had been sung. Popcorn that Harry made the old-fashioned way, clapping a dish towel over the pot lid to muffle the sound, propping open the kitchen window so the smell wouldn't drift upstairs where the children, we hoped, were sleeping. Something about that popcorn drove me wild. The odor of melting butter. The hot kernels bursting on my tongue. There were nights when we barely made it to the couch, our hands reaching deep into the open mouth of the bowl, grease searing our fingers, salt crystals sticking to our lips. Afterward, drowsy, we'd sink back into the sofa cushions and watch reruns of *The Bob Newhart Show,* seeking out the occasional dropped kernel from the folds of our rumpled clothing. All I had to do was smile at him a certain way and Harry would rise to the occasion and pop up another batch.

Did I overpraise him just a bit? Did I tell him his popcorn was the best I'd ever eaten? Did I make it clear he'd ruined me for all popcorn made by another man's hand?

You bet I did. It's called Positive Reinforcement. And though it never seemed to have much of an effect on the kids, it certainly worked on Harry.

One night, he surprised me with brownies from a mix that he'd doctored with nuts and chocolate chips. Next came a series of cheesecakes. Then there was that very first batch of Toll House cookies—a memorable event for us both. He began to putter around the kitchen after supper while I wrestled Amber and the twins into their jammies. "How many teaspoons in a tablespoon?" he'd holler up the stairs, or "When it says to 'scald' something, does that mean burn it?" He'd run up to kiss the children with sugary lips, leaving smudges of flour in their hair, before racing back down in case something had set, something had boiled, the timer had gone off.

"Grown-up food," I told the girls, who raised their little pink noses suspiciously from their pillows. "Nasty. Yuck."

Then I hurried after him to warm up the couch. The moment *Newhart* came on, I'd call out, "Hi, Bob!" which was Harry's cue to appear with something delicious on a plate.

Back in the era known to us as B.C. (Before Children), we'd occasionally played a little drinking game, taking a shot whenever one of the Newhart characters called out, "Hi, Bob!" Now we played "Hi, Bob!" with bites of chocolate-bourbon pie, or Brie baked in a pastry shell, or chunks of lemon-poppyseed cake chased down with made-from-scratch peach ginger ale. And Harry's newfound culinary interests didn't stop there. I began coming home from work to find, for example, mustard-glazed slices of pork accompanied by organic hearts of romaine; crispy duck breasts in a pear-and-mango chutney; spicy shrimp shish kebabs sizzling over the grill attachment that I'd never learned to use.

Discovering such things on my dining room table was a little like discovering a van Gogh at a yard sale. You didn't ask how and why it had come to be there, you just grabbed the thing and ran. Not that I was a bad cook, exactly. The meals I'd thrown together since our marriage began had always approximated the Food Pyramid, but they'd also left us feeling as if we were eating the same things over and over again. Meat. Potato. Rice. Something that had once been green, cooked or creamed beyond recognition. Dessert from a box, carton, or snack cup. I cooked the way my mother had cooked—to get it over with. Let other moms simmer their soups and pinch their pies. Mine was quick to let you know she'd been put on this earth for better things. Ignorant cavewomen stood barefoot and pregnant over the fire, but modern gals shopped the frozen-food aisles, programmed their microwaves, and got the job done.

It had never occurred to me that there were people in the world who approached a meal the way a painter approaches a canvas. Like Mom, I'd look at a raw lamb chop and think, If I cut it into bite-sized pieces, it'll cook faster. Harry looked at the very same chop and thought, Shallots, minced, with elephant garlic and red wine. And then he made it happen. I noticed he was getting fuller in the belly, wider in the hips—and mind you, he'd never been skinny to begin with—but he was happy. *I* was happy. It was 1979. What woman would have complained when, in a world of husbands who didn't even *help* with the cooking, yours decided he was going to be a man and do his share? And I admired Harry all the more because he didn't come from an equal-opportunity household. In the Kligler family, Man said grace, and Wife did everything else. I have seen, with my own eyes, the sight of Mathilde Kligler in a restaurant, leaning across the table to cut up her husband's meat.

"Is Daddy cooking tonight?" Amber and the twins had asked as soon as they could speak English. All three of the girls had been early talkers, but they'd spoken in a strange, pseudo twin-speak I never managed to decode. I doubt they'd have learned the mother tongue at all if they hadn't wanted their father to feed them.

"He'll cook," I'd say, "but only if you girls are very, very good."

Weekends, he'd spend entire afternoons in the kitchen, experimenting with various breads: crusty loaves smelling of rosemary and thyme, buttery dinner rolls, sticky buns drowning in pecans. He planted an herb garden. He purchased springform pans and pizza stones; he enrolled in weekend seminars on cake decorating, Northern Italian cuisine, the Wines of Spain. I watched it all with a growing sense of awe. Harry was—I'll be frank—a computer geek, a tech-head, the sort of person who stuttered with excitement at the mention of a binary system. He was also hopelessly, brutally shy. He hid behind his computer screen in the same way, I suspect, he'd have hidden behind a cleric's collar and long black robe. So what motivated such a man to rise early on a Saturday to tenderly proof a batch of sourdough? How had he mustered the nerve to befriend our ornery butcher, flattering him into offering us the best cuts of meat? Where had he learned to garnish a pie with a twist of orange peel, or a strawberry, sliced and fanned? How did he know that the effect was called presentation?

Harry seemed surprised that I was surprised.

"I read, Francie," he said, in his mild way. "I learn. I pick things up as I go."

But I didn't think it was that simple. No, his culinary talent was a calling. *This* was the vocation he'd been praying for when he'd written to Pittsburgh Seminary.

"I can't believe you didn't use a recipe," I said one night after taking a bite of his latest invention: seared scallops encrusted with black truffle shavings. "You *couldn't* have invented this from scratch."

Harry smiled his best altar boy smile.

"For those who believe," he said, "no explanation is necessary. For those who do not believe, no explanation is possible."

*   *   *

EVERY POSITIVE HAS its negative; every yin has its yang. Harry's waistline grew in step with his culinary accomplishments.

At this point I should admit that I am a physical therapist. A physical therapist, of all people, should know what to say when, every spring, her beloved pulls out the shorts he'd bought on sale the previous fall and announces that they must have shrunk in the wash. A physical therapist should see right through such wishful thinking and denounce it, then and there. After all, it isn't likely that shorts with crisp, bright tags still attached have shrunk in the wash. It is far more likely that the beloved is living in a world of his own making, a delusional world in which he remains the same size while everything around him gets smaller: airline seats, restaurant chairs, swimming trunks.

If Harry had been referred to me as a patient, I would have known exactly how to burst his bubble. I would have done it kindly, but briskly, like stripping off a Band-Aid stuck to a plump inner thigh. I would have pointed out that he'd been gaining five to seven pounds a year. I would have frightened him with promises of diabetes and heart disease, stroke and colon cancer. I would have shown him photographs of deteriorating knee joints, edemic ankles, amputated toes. Then I would have marched him to the nearest stationary bike and told him I wanted to see those knees pumping.

But the person I was every day from eight till four at Pittsburgh Family Medical—a competent person, if I do say so myself—was not the same person I became at five past four, when I got in my car and headed back home, wondering what delightful confection Harry had planned for dessert. *Do as I say, but not as I do.* It's older than Shakespeare, older than Moses, perhaps even older than God. The person who ripped off countless Band-Aids with ease found herself unable to suggest that, perhaps, her beloved shouldn't be having second helpings of the veal and spinach lasagna, that he definitely shouldn't be finishing the meal with an enormous bowl of cappuccino gelato, that he certainly didn't need to eat fingerfuls of Devon cream straight from the jar before bed. Of course, I had excuses. For one thing, Mathilde Kligler was the size of a small ship, and yet—she'd be the first to tell you this—her cholesterol was "perfect." Wasn't it quite possible that Harry was genetically pro-grammed to run on the heavy side? Another thing: He carried his weight extremely well. People sometimes said he looked a bit like Brian Dennehy, which I was happy to take as a compliment. But the main reason I kept silent was this: Harry's weight had been a sensitive topic since his childhood. He'd always been chubby, picked last for every team, the bashful boy who sat by himself on the school bus. At home, his weight had sparked countless fights at the Kligler dinner table, with Mathilde slip-ping second helpings onto his plate even as Harry Senior threat-ened to send him away to a military-style fat camp in the Adirondacks.

Why compound the injuries of youth? Harry knew he was overweight without me reminding him of the fact whenever he lifted a fork or a finger. Besides, wasn't stress more dangerous than all the other evils put together? At least Harry was happy. He was easygoing, laid-back. His idea of a perfect Saturday night was to cuddle up on the couch with me and browse through the latest issue of *Gourmet*. Cooking, eating, experi-menting with recipes, inviting friends and family to share the results—this was how Harry relaxed.

By the time we conceived Jason, the kitchen had become Harry's kingdom. Pots and pans I'd always thrown into the gritty metal drawer beneath the oven were hanging from their own special rack on the wall, polished copper bottoms shining like moons above an unfamiliar planet. Drawers were lined with Con-Tact paper. Wooden spoons were separated from the paring knives. The ancient, graying spices had disappeared, replaced by fresh, exotic varieties ordered from All-Clad. The cupboards bulged with hazelnut flour, dehydrated egg whites, rose water, citrus oils. An apron hung inside the broom closet, adorned with a pair of red lips and the words KISS THE COOK—AND I DON'T MEAN MY WIFE! From time to time, I still cooked a few of my Food Pyramid meals, which I hoped—hopelessly—would offset Harry's elaborate desserts and buttery sauces.

But even that came to an end when I entered my final trimester.

Amber and the twins—so difficult in life—had entered it with barely a twinge. I suffered no morning sickness, no bloating. No esophageal reflux. No sciatica. Even labor was remarkably unremarkable. Both times, my water broke within a day of my due date. Contractions politely held off until we reached the hospital. There was the sting of the epidural and then, four or five hours later, presto! A baby (or two) arrived. And not a single stretch mark afterward. What, I wondered, was all the fuss about? Having a baby wasn't any worse than having your tonsils out.

Jason—so much kinder and gentler than his sisters—blistered me with nausea. He drove my blood pressure through the roof. He jackhammered my kidneys. During the thirty-third week, we sent the girls across town to Harry's parents, and I took a medical leave from work. For the next two weeks, I lay on my left side, swelling like a melon as Harry murmured comforting things. It would have seemed petty to mention that Harry was swelling like a melon, too. Every night, he brought me my supper on a wicker tray, and on that tray was a small white vase that never failed to hold a flower, and beside that vase was a discreetly folded paper lunch bag in case I needed to vomit.

"I'm so sorry about this, Francie," he told me, as if it were his fault. Which, in a roundabout way, I suppose it was. "If I could trade places with you, I swear I would."

Dear Harry. I had to ask myself: Was it such a bad thing that there was more of him to love?

After the C-section, I never even cracked another egg, though I always was a sport and did the dishes. Harry cooked for me, and he cooked for Amber and the twins, and as soon as Jason got big enough, he cooked for Jason as well. He baked for PTA meetings and Valentine's Day parties, spring picnics and summer barbecues—events that, once, he would have tried to avoid, blaming anything from a headache to a hangnail. Now he was the center of attention as he carried in the hors d'oeuvres. Neighbors began hanging over the hedges to chat whenever Harry fired up the grill, tangy smells wafting up and down the street like a beckoning finger. There was always plenty to share: orange-marinated ribs, potato salad with walnuts and pickles, watermelon soaked in rum, and, of course, a layer cake or two.

Our neighborhood is a colorful mix of different folks, each of us dwelling in a house or duplex that battles architecturally with everything else on the street. Only red meat and sugar could have broken through our mutual reserve and turned us all into back-door friends. There were John and Krys Placek, children of first-generation Polish-Americans, who were raising their own daughters to be bilingual; there was old Mr. Polk, a retired army officer from Tuscaloosa; there were Mari Diaz and Beth Taylor, whose VW bug boasted bumper stickers reading WITCHES HEAL and WOMEN NEED MEN LIKE FISH NEED BICYCLES. Last, but never least, there was Malva Miracle—yes, her real name—who claimed Nigerian and Cherokee descent, "plus a whole lot of colonialist savagery." She showed up one day with a tall, handsome boy whom she introduced as her son, Malvin.

Malvin looked at Amber and flashed her a lightning smile.

Amber put her hands on her hips and flashed him some lightning of her own.

The moment came to be known, in neighborhood lore, as the Big Bang.

Eventually, those first casual summer get-togethers evolved into full-fledged dinner parties at which Harry played the magnanimous chef—and I was the scullery maid. Everyone, even Mari and Beth, said how "lucky" I was as I stood in the kitchen afterward, hand-washing the seventy-odd pans Harry had needed to make his exquisite tapas. I agreed, of course, though I suspected they'd have said the same thing if I had cooked the meals and *Harry* had done the dishes. We may have come a long way, baby, but the eighties and nineties weren't all that different from the fifties when it came to domestic roles. If a man carried his plate to the sink, people still fell to their knees.

More of that Positive Reinforcement, I guess.

In this way, time passed. Amber left for college, followed by the twins. Harry left his comfy old job to work for a high-tech spin-off company, lured by the whisper of stock options. Amber got married and moved to London. Amber got divorced and returned to the condo she'd been sharing with Malvin downtown. The twins spent a year living at opposite ends of the country to prove, as they put it, "we *are* two separate people, named Tina and Trish"—and then announced they were opening a hemp clothing store in Burlington, Vermont. Jason astonished everyone by revealing an IQ that had Mensa in a flutter. The neighborhood celebrated the millennium in our dining room with a Mexican feast, complete with a piñata that Mari and the Placek girls had made out of papier-mâché.

Now and then, Harry would fret about his weight. He'd

stand in front of the mirror, tucking and untucking. He'd try to touch his toes. He'd ask me if I thought he was getting, uh, you know, fat, and the look in his eyes made it clear that diplomacy was called for. He was, once again, sitting all by himself on the school bus. He was waiting, without hope, to get picked for the team. He was listening to Harry Senior describe the rigors of the fat camp, where you had to hike for ten miles before you got your breakfast.

Gently, I agreed that, well, yes, he'd probably gained a few more pounds since the last time he'd asked. Perhaps we could start taking a walk after dinner. After all, I wouldn't mind losing ten pounds myself. I mentioned a few easy exercises we could do together. I talked about free weights. I even suggested we join a gym.

Harry nodded agreeably.

But by the time the evening meal rolled around, we'd be tucking into our goat-cheese-and-basil pierogi—Krys Placek's recipe—as if the subject had never come up. And after dinner? Well, these days it was *Seinfeld* reruns. I mean, who wants to miss *Seinfeld*?

I have no doubt that we would have carried on in exactly the same way, sledding recklessly down the steep hill of Time, eyes squinched tight against the elements, if we hadn't hit a tree.

That tree was a holiday raffle prize in the form of a deluxe digitized bathroom scale.

PART ONE

Two Hundred Sixty-nine Pounds

I did not attend Harry's company's annual Holiday Raffle. Spouses and partners were never invited. Harry's company believed that restricting company-sanctioned gatherings to employees encouraged *collegial bonding.* This always seemed to me like a euphemism for *extramarital affairs,* though Harry assured me it wasn't.

"It's just dot-com nonsense, Francie," he said, pulling on his coat and patting the pockets for his keys. "Some business psychologist told them to do it, so they do."

He stood by the door, shifting from foot to foot, jingling his change. He always got nervous before he had to go to a party. "Too many adults walking around unattended," was how he explained it. But everybody in the company had to participate in the Holiday Raffle. You had to sign in with the office manager to prove that you'd been there.

Harry's company was so uptight I wasn't even allowed so say what it was he did, other than "computers." There was more and more talk of the company stock going public, but I wasn't supposed to say that, either. The company was an Internet spin-off of the staid and stodgy company where Harry had worked for nearly twenty years. At forty-three, he'd been the oldest employee to make the leap. Now, at forty-seven, he was the one the twenty-something dot-cowboys were referring to when they whispered, "It wouldn't hurt to have some white hair in on the deal." Enter Harry, familiar as a slice of Wonder Bread in his conservative tie, his wandering hairline, his solid mass of reassurance. The clients signed on the dot-com line. The cowboys high-fived one another over the tops of their cubicles.

"That's the only time they listen to me," Harry complained now, the change in his pockets jingling like sleigh bells. "When they think something might fall through. As soon as things are back on track, they hustle me out of the picture."

"Why? You've got more experience than any of them."

"That's the problem." More sleigh bells. "To them, anybody over thirty is ancient. They call me Father Time. And that's what they call me to my face."

"Say something," I urged him, even though I knew he wouldn't. Harry wasn't big on confronting people. Sure enough, even the possibility was making him uncomfortable. He turned to open the door.

"Ah, well. They're only kids." He winced at the blast of cold air. "Deep down, they love me, right?"

"They love your cookies, anyway."

"Cookies." The thought seemed to cheer him. "I'll be back as soon as I can."

I, for one, was talking about the actual, edible kind of cookie—known in company parlance as *literal cookies*—as opposed to the cyberspace cookies that they were all busily coding and decoding. On hump days—that is, Wednesdays—Harry always brought in four or five dozen *literals* and reheated them in batches in the office microwave. Many were his own inspired recipes: Helplessly Chocolate, Peppermint Power, Coconut Monkey Faces. The Peanutbetter Butterbursts, however, remained everybody's favorite, and the aroma never failed to lure the cowboys in from the flat-screened fields. They elbowed one another out of the way like the children they still were. They chewed with their mouths open. They tried to sneak handfuls back to their workstations, which had been forbidden ever since crumbs had gotten into a keyboard and made it go berserk. Harry liked to describe the scene in the voice-over tones of a nature documentary, even though he'd signed a confidentiality statement promising not to discuss anything that happened at work.

I tell you these things as a way of saying that it was no sacrifice to stay home from the Holiday Raffle, which always began with upbeat group exercises in cooperative thinking and mutual trust. Last year, the employees had to build some kind of scaffolding and help one another climb over it. Fortunately, Harry hadn't been quite to the top when the thing collapsed. Everybody had been very, very nice, he'd told me later, on the way to the emergency room. This year, rumor had it that employees were supposed to take turns standing on chairs and falling backward into one another's arms. Harry's waist was now a tight forty-two.

I just didn't want to think about it.

So as soon as his car pulled out of the driveway, I got to work decorating the house for the holidays. It was the first year we'd be relatively on our own. Tina and Trish were volunteering with Habitat for Humanity. Amber had flown to Jamaica with Malvin, declaring that December in Pittsburgh and suicide were synonymous. My mother, who had retired to Florida, begged off with the promise of attending Jason's high-school graduation in June, when the weather was civilized. At least

Jason was still around, studying upstairs in his room, but who could say where he'd be next year? He was graduating at the top of his class, one year ahead of schedule. College recruiters had been calling nonstop; Cornell and Stanford had already offered scholarships. At seventeen, he'd be gone. It would be just Harry and me. There'd be time for hobbies. Weekend getaways. Maybe even those gym memberships. And on the horizon? Retirement. Travel. A couple of grandkids. An RV with one of those waving yellow signs in the window: CAUTION: I'M SPENDING MY CHILDREN'S INHERITANCE.

Frankly, it didn't sound half bad.

I polished the menorah from my daddy's side of the family and set it on the dining room table. I scattered foil-wrapped chocolate coins across the mantel for gelt, even though I knew that Harry would just eat them. Then I hauled the artificial Christmas tree down from the attic in honor of my mother's Baptist kin. I vacuumed away the cobwebs, untangled the various strings of lights, and fitted them with multicolored fish of no particular denomination. Finally, I dug out the enormous Christmas clock that Harry's parents had given Amber when she was just a year old. Its face was—what else?— Santa Claus's face, and every time the hour struck, an awful mechanized voice chortled, "Ho-Ho-Ho!" It overwhelmed my daddy's lovely old menorah like a condominium complex beside a turn-of-the-century Victorian. I hated the thing, but the kids had always adored it. To them, it was part of the holiday season, like spinning the dreidel, like eggnog and fruitcake.

I was studying the Christmas tree, debating the tinsel issue, when Jason came down the stairs.

"You put up the tree," he said reproachfully. "I would have helped, you know."

"I knew you were studying."

"I could have taken a break."

"Sorry, Pop-Tart."

Harry's old nickname for Jason had stuck, but Jason didn't seem to mind. Regardless of test scores, he would always be Pop-Tart to his family.

The Santa Claus clock chimed ten P.M. "Ho-Ho-Ho! Ho-Ho-Ho! Ho-Ho-Ho! Ho!" I watched Jason's head snap around. His mouth opened into a little round *Ho!* of his own beneath the wispy mustache he'd been trying to grow for a year.

"Aw, the Santa Claus clock!" he said, forgiving me everything. "I *love* that clock."

"I know."

"The tree needs tinsel, don't you think?"

"I was actually thinking of stringing popcorn instead."

"I'll make it," he said, heading for the kitchen. "Dad still out?"

"Yup."

"Isn't he late?"

"A little."

"Think he got hurt again?"

"I hope not."

Jason shook the heavy pan as the kernels rattled and popped. He had his father's way with popcorn; the smell was heavenly.

"Let's put butter on that batch," I said, digging through the junk drawer for the sewing kit. "We can always make more for stringing."

"Don't worry, I made plenty." Jason threw a whole stick of butter in a bowl and stuck it in the microwave. To look at him, you'd never have guessed that he came from a family that did not believe in margarine. He was so thin that it made me want to apologize. I suspected his accelerated brain was leaching necessary minerals from his body.

"I wonder if Dad'll win anything this year," he mused.

I'll say this for Harry's company: Their raffle prizes were extraordinary. Many were prototypes for things you still couldn't buy on the market.

"I could go for the flat-screened portable TV," I said.

Jason made a face. "I hope he wins the robo-dog."

"I hope he does *not* win the robo-dog!"

"Aw, Mom, you'd love it. I'd program it to get your slippers."

"I don't wear slippers."

"I'd program it to follow you around and keep you company."

Jason saved a small dish of popcorn for stringing, then shook the rest into the same bowl Harry and I had shared for so many years. He dumped the butter in with a splash and carried everything to the table. I handed him a needle, already threaded.

"The *last* thing I need," I said, stabbing a hot kernel, "is some little mechanical thing following me around. I spent too many years with little human things following me around."

Jason was more interested in eating popcorn than in stringing it. He filled his mouth with an impossibly large handful, then studied me, crunching. Since his babyhood, he'd looked somber, thoughtful, even when he was smiling, and he wasn't smiling now.

"What?" I said.

"You're going to be lonely," he said. "After I'm gone. So will Dad."

"You won't be *gone,* you'll be in college," I protested, though it was exactly what I'd been thinking earlier. Jason had a way of listening in on people's thoughts. You'd think to yourself, I'm kind of thirsty, and he'd appear with a glass of water. It was unnerving.

"You may experience mild to moderate depression," Jason said, adopting a formal tone. "You might start to question fundamental assumptions. Basic values could appear subjective."

"In other words, I'll be reaching for the Prozac?"

"Don't laugh," he said, shaking his head disapprovingly. "While it's true that professionals often dismiss the plight of the empty nester, the syndrome is a genuine phase-of-life transition with genuine consequences. It's best to be prepared."

I stared at my mathematically brilliant, hopelessly earnest son. In many ways, he seemed younger than seventeen. He was planning a career in quantitative psychology, which I gathered had something to do with creating statistical programs on computers to map the impulses of the human brain—after getting his M.D., of course. I imagined him in his high-school cafeteria with the athletes and the potheads, immune to their curiosity and scorn, quantum physics and pop psychology dancing like sugarplum fairies in his head. At six, seeing me unplug the vacuum with a yank of the cord, he explained why it was safer to grasp the plug, elaborating on the conductive nature of electricity. I could see that same six-year-old in him now, and I wanted to embrace him, but you don't do that to a teenage boy—even a boy like Jason, who prided himself on being free of what he called *Oedipal angst.*

"Around that same time," he continued soberly, "it is likely

Dad will have a midlife crisis. Mom, don't laugh. It's hormonal. His testosterone levels will drop. There's nothing funny about it."

"I'm sure there isn't," I said, stringing popcorn madly.

"It may be happening already," Jason continued. "Have you noticed he's looking kind of, you know, puffy?"

"Puffy?"

Jason nodded. "That can be one of the signs. Hormones affect metabolism. Any idea how much he weighs these days?"

I shook my head. I thought I'd been the only one who'd noticed that, after years of slow creepage, Harry's weight had been rising exponentially. I'd been planning to say something to him about it, too, as soon as the holidays were out of the way. He always ate more around the holidays. He also ate more whenever he was bored, or unhappy, or nervous about something, or—especially—working long hours. Lately, since the dot-coms had been strafed by reality, he'd been putting in ten-hour days—all the surviving dot-cowboys did the same. But they were twenty years younger than Harry. Perhaps he was simply feeling his age. On weekends, he seemed to be sleeping more and more. Napping in the afternoon. Falling asleep on the couch after dinner. He was oddly . . . sluggish. Puffy, too. But it had been a particularly dark and dreary fall. Everyone in Pittsburgh was sluggish and puffy.

"Maybe he's just been eating too much." I was still trying to keep things light.

"But the question is why?" Jason said. "For physiological reasons? Is he craving some vital fatty oil to regulate his amino acids? Or perhaps . . ."

"Perhaps what?"

"Perhaps he's been seeking emotional solace in food."

"Or perhaps he's just been eating too much," I repeated.

"People don't 'just eat too much.'" Jason fixed me with a paternal stare. "Are you and Dad, you know, okay?"

"Jason!" I didn't know whether to laugh or be offended. After twenty-four years, Harry and I weren't exactly honeymooners, but still. We enjoyed each other's company. We never fought. Sometimes we even held hands at the mall. "Of course we're okay."

"What about his job?"

They call me Father Time. "Jason, please, everything's fine."

"Maybe this involves latent childhood issues. In my opinion, Gramma Kligler was awfully overprotective, and Grampa—"

With relief, I heard Harry's car pull into the drive. "Hey, I think I hear the Hormonally Imbalanced One now."

Jason looked at me sympathetically. "Mom," he said. "Just remember I'm always here for you. I mean, if you ever want to talk."

"Thank you," I said, as soberly as I could.

"Don't mention it."

"Hello?" Harry shouted from the entryway, and not a moment too soon.

"What did we win?" I called back.

"Just a minute and I'll show you." We could hear him taking off his coat.

"The robo-dog?" Jason said, his voice cracking with excitement.

But when Harry padded into the room, he was carrying a flat, square box. Thankfully, he didn't look like a man who'd spent the past few hours falling backward off a chair.

"What's that?" Jason asked.

Harry handed it over. "Not the dog. Sorry, Pop-Tart."

"Can I open it?" he asked.

"Sure." Harry observed the tree. "Needs tinsel, don't you think?"

Jason was already inside the box. " 'The New You Digital Scale with Select Vocalizations,' " he read out loud. "Hey, a new scale! Just what we need around here."

He gave me a thumbs-up behind his father's back.

"It was the prize *next* to the TV," Harry said. "Can you believe it?"

"You were robbed," I consoled him, ignoring Jason.

"I tried to trade it for a sonic foot massager."

"You did the best you could."

"No, wait, Dad, this is really cool," Jason said, flipping the box to read the back. "It's got one of those learning chips. You have to program it."

His eyes glittered the way they did whenever something needed to be programmed.

"Be my guest," Harry told him. He sat down with an *oomph* and started in on the popcorn. "What an evening."

"How can a bathroom scale learn?" I asked Jason.

"It remembers your profile. You know, how much you weighed the last time, what your ideal weight should be, that kind of thing. And then it responds accordingly." Already he had the thing out of the box and was pushing buttons. "Hey, Dad?" His voice was innocent. "When you weigh yourself, do you want to hear a male or female voice?"

There was a beat of silence. The idea of Harry weighing himself—well, Harry simply didn't weigh himself. Whenever I'd murmured about replacing the scale the girls had broken, Harry said there was no need, he didn't want a scale cluttering up the bathroom. Yes, he knew he'd put on a few pounds, but he didn't require a scale to figure that out. Besides, he could always get weighed when he had his next physical. The problem was that this physical never came. Harry hadn't been to see a doctor for the past ten years.

"What's the point?" he'd say when I brought up the subject. "I don't need a doctor to tell me I'm overweight." More than once, I tried to convince him to drop by Pittsburgh Family Medical to see Tommy Choi, one of the doctors I worked with. Tommy had the Midas touch when it came to the difficult, the nervous, the white-lipped—in other words, people who hated doctors. Besides, he and I had become pals after his daughter fractured her ankle, a complicated injury involving months of ongoing physical therapy. Sue-Sue had adored me. Now Tommy adored me, too. He had told me more than once that he'd be happy to "give Harry a tune-up" any time Harry wanted one.

But Harry was having none of it. "He's just going to tell me I need to lose weight. I *know* I need to lose weight. I don't need an M.D. to tell me that, all right?"

There were very few subjects that made Harry irritable.

This one was the eight ball.

So when Jason asked Harry if he wanted to hear a male or female voice when he weighed himself, it was a loaded question. No matter how Harry answered, he'd be, in effect, agreeing to step on the scale. By stepping on the scale, he'd be forcing himself to confront the numerical evidence of his weight gain. Such a confrontation might very well lead to actual, concrete steps toward a remedy. Steps like, say, a doctor's appointment. A modified diet. Regular exercise. Or—I couldn't help thinking about what Jason had said—figuring out why he was overeating in the first place. There was some kind of complex psychological name for what Jason was doing, I was quite certain of it. But his expression was open and earnest as always. He was going to make one hell of an excellent quantitative psychologist.

Harry said, "Female."

"Young or old?" Jason said.

"Young." Harry, it seemed, was willing to play.

"How do you feel about humor?"

"Humor's good," Harry said.

Jason punched some more buttons.

"You wouldn't believe what they had us doing tonight," Harry told me. "The theme was 'working together.' We had to run relay races with raw eggs balanced on spoons."

"We used to do that in Brownies," I said.

"I pity whoever has to clean it all up."

"Hey, pay attention," Jason said. "Sex Kitten or Drill Master?"

"What?"

"Mom, I'm just reading what it says."

Harry gave Jason a look that said, *Duh*. "Kitten, of course."

"Now watch," Jason said. He tapped the scale twice and the digital window flashed. When it stopped, a seductive female voice said, "Hop on, big guy."

Harry burst out laughing.

"I don't believe this," I said.

Jason obeyed. "One hundred thirty-seven pounds," the voice cooed. "A bit on the *slender* side for my taste."

The voice laughed wickedly. So did Harry and Jason.

"How can it know what your weight range should be?" I protested.

"Because when you set up your profile, you enter in how old you are, how tall you are, that kind of thing."

"Well, the *last* thing I want when I step on a scale," I said, "is some computer chip calling me *big girl*."

"But Mom, it *won't*," Jason said in the very patient voice he used when explaining something to the computer illiterate. "This isn't your profile. Your profile would be different. Now watch this."

He looked around the room, then headed for the bay window. Years earlier, he'd sprouted an avocado pit for some school project, and we'd made the mistake of planting the thing. Now it was three feet tall and clearly aspiring to greater heights. Jason picked it up and lugged it over to the scale.

Tap tap.

"Ready for ya, big guy," the scale said.

"Didn't it say something else before?" I said.

"That's what I'm trying to tell you," Jason said. "It's got, like, a personality. It learns. But this is just the quick-start program. That's why we'll be able to trick it." He stepped up, still holding the avocado plant.

There was a pause.

"Uh-oh!" the scale said sternly. "One hundred sixty-one pounds. *You* have been a *very* naughty boy."

This time I laughed, too.

"The advanced setup will know how much time has passed, if it's your morning or evening weight, that kind of thing," Jason said. "But we don't need any of that now." He was pushing buttons again. "Now I'm resetting the profile for Dad. How tall are you again?"

"Five foot ten," Harry said.

Five feet and eight inches worth of that statement were true. Jason must have known this, too, but he let it pass.

"Now encircle your wrist with your thumb and first finger. Do they meet?"

Harry looked alarmed. "What if they don't?"

"It means you have a large bone structure, that's all. Your ideal weight allowance will be higher."

"Oh," Harry said, mollified. "They don't meet."

"Large bone structure," Jason said, entering it in. "Okay. She's ready for you, Dad."

Harry looked uneasy.

"Stop calling the bathroom scale 'she,'" I said, stalling. It had occurred to me that Harry might not want the lead role in a public performance. "Look, Jason, Dad can do this some other time."

"No, it's okay," Harry said. He stood up. "I mean, how bad can this be? I probably weigh—what? One ninety, one ninety-five?"

I tried to look noncommittal. I was thinking two thirty, two thirty-five.

"One way to find out," Jason said.

Harry tapped the scale twice.

"Hop on, big guy," the scale purred.

"I thought it was supposed to say something new," I said.

"I reset it for Dad," Jason said. "It starts over."

"I don't like to be kept waiting," the scale said petulantly.

Obediently, Harry stood on the scale.

"Two hundred sixty-nine pounds," the scale said. "Your maximum ideal weight is one hundred and sixty pounds. *You* have been a *very* naughty boy."

The Christmas clock chose this moment to strike.

"Ho-Ho-Ho!" it cried. "Ho-Ho-Ho! Ho-Ho-Ho! Ho-Ho!"

"Jesus," Harry finally said. "I'm a hundred pounds overweight."

I was shocked, too. At work, I could eyeball nearly any patient's weight with a fair degree of accuracy. But Harry just looked like Harry to me, only bigger.

"Francie?" he said. "I don't *look* like I'm one hundred pounds overweight, do I?"

I never got a chance to answer. Footsteps pounded up the porch steps. The back door flew open. Amber burst into the entryway, a duffel bag over her shoulder. Her nose was sunburned. Her eyes were red and wild. Her blond hair was braided into a dozen springy pigtails that stuck out like exclamation points.

"Men *suck*!" she announced, kicking off her shoes with such force, we heard them bounce off the wall.

Then she looked up and saw us: Harry, frozen on the scale like a god on a pedestal, Jason and I staring up at him.

"Hi, Daddy," she said, sweetly. "What on earth are you doing?"

Harry stepped off the scale.

"Hello, Dumpling," he said.

2

We were all surprised to see Amber, of course, but nobody was shocked. Harry called her our boomerang child. Time after time, she'd fling herself out into the world, only to crash-land back on our doorstep after a month, a week, a year. She'd appeared after dropping out of Penn State two months shy of a degree in something called, vaguely, Communications and Society. She'd reappeared after the breakup of her marriage to a British business tycoon thirty years her senior. These days, she showed up whenever she and Malvin had one of their spectacular fallings-out. This latest one, like all the others, was *it,* the very last straw. She'd left him in Jamaica, she couldn't recall exactly where, sipping piña coladas under a hotel cabana. Back in their room, she'd filled the Jacuzzi and submerged all his possessions—with the exception of his passport and airline ticket. These she'd shredded with her nail scissors and scattered across the bed. She told us everything between athletic hugs and kisses.

"Man, that's harsh," Jason said, impressed. "What's he going to do?"

"He's a bright man," Amber said crisply. "He'll figure something out." She gave an explosive sigh, as if she were exhaling the last remnants of Malvin forever. "So! I'm parched! Anything to drink?"

While Harry went to the kitchen to whip up a little of his signature eggnog, Jason put the scale underneath the Christmas tree.

"I feel terrible," he whispered.

"It's okay," I said. "You didn't mean to upset him."

"That isn't what I meant," Jason said, giving me an unfriendly look. "Mom, aren't you scared? He's, like, *seriously* overweight."

I realized my mistake. "Well, we didn't need a scale to tell us that," I said, sounding every bit as defensive as Harry.

"What are you hush-hushing about?" Amber called from the doorway. "Malvin's history, okay? I mean it this time, so you can stop speculating."

As usual, it was difficult to concentrate on anything other than Amber when Amber was home.

In the kitchen, I had a sociable glass of eggnog as Amber told us all about Malvin's indifference, Malvin's arrogance, Malvin's inability to explain certain hotel receipts. It was all fine with Amber. She couldn't care less. She'd move back into her old room until she found a place of her own, maybe one of those sweet Tudors over in Squirrel Hill, something with lots of brick and natural wood and sunlight. Let Malvin have his chilly designs, his otherworldly furniture. Let Malvin keep the whole damn condo, those cool tile floors and stainless-steel surfaces. *She* was a human being. Human beings need color, texture, warmth. Not to mention a straight answer once in a while.

"More eggnog?" Harry said, but Amber didn't seem to hear.

"Honesty," she told Jason, placing a smooth, tanned hand over his. "That's the key ingredient, 'Tart. Don't you ever forget it."

Jason nodded, a rapt expression on his face. As far as I knew, he had yet to have a single date. "Honesty," he repeated.

The Santa Claus clock chimed midnight, and Amber stopped talking to listen. "Aw, the Christmas clock!" she cried. "I *love* that clock!"

"I'm pooped," Harry said, taking the opportunity to get to his feet. "It's late for an old man like me. I'll see you in the morning, Dumpling, okay?"

He kissed Amber's forehead, thumped Jason's shoulder, then headed up to bed without even looking at me. I couldn't help but notice that he'd had not one but two glasses of eggnog, and that he'd also eaten the lion's share of the Christmas cookies he'd put out for Amber and Jason. Immediately, I hated myself for registering these things. I reminded myself that he was the same person he'd been *before* I knew how much he weighed. And yet the scale had changed everything. Harry's weight was no longer a nebulous cloud, the thing on the horizon you tried not to mention, like a thundercloud that appears during the sunniest of picnics. The thundercloud was overhead. It had broken open above us: We couldn't ignore it anymore. I thought of the future I'd imagined for us both just a few hours earlier: the hobbies, the travel. I heard Jason's voice in my head: *Aren't you scared?*

"I'm turning in, too," I said. "It's good to see you, Amber, even though . . ."

I never knew what to say after she broke up with Malvin. If I said I was sorry, she would look annoyed and say there was nothing to be sorry about. But I couldn't pretend I was happy about the thought of Malvin in Jamaica, trying to explain things to the concierge, wearing only his swim trunks and a smile. I liked Malvin. He could be a scoundrel, yes, but Amber could be a scoundrel, too. It was Malvin she'd been living with up until the night before she married the British business tycoon.

"Thanks, Mom," Amber said, letting me off the hook.

In the living room, I turned off all the lights, except the multicolored fishes. Beneath the Christmas tree, the scale was shining like a patch of black ice. I should have seen it coming, I thought. I shouldn't have let Jason set Harry up. I should have simply left the scale in the bathroom—the guest bathroom— where Harry could have weighed himself in his own good time, not to mention with a lot more privacy. What good could come out of this kind of ambush? All it had accomplished was to make him feel particularly awful about himself. A person with a poor self-image doesn't run out to buy jogging shoes. He opens the freezer and sticks his head into a bucket of Butter Pecan.

In Harry's case, he'd churn his own, with extra nuts.

I was heading toward the stairs to join him, steeling myself against what I knew would be a difficult conversation, when I heard Amber say, "What's wrong with the P.U.s? Did they have a fight or something?"

P.U. stood for Parental Units, by which my darling meant her father and me.

I started to call out, "No, we did *not* have a fight!" But then, for some reason, I didn't. Instead, I kept perfectly still, listening to Jason explain about the Holiday Raffle and the New You Digital Scale.

"So what does Dad weigh now, anyway?" Amber asked. "He must be close to three hundred."

My heart sank: Did he really look that big? I reminded myself that Amber had always been prone to exaggeration.

"Almost two seventy," Jason said glumly.

"God, what a whale."

"Don't call Dad a whale," Jason said.

I made a mental note to let Jason borrow the car whenever he wanted.

"You want me to be politically correct? He's metabolically challenged, how's that?"

"That's better than a whale."

Amber seemed to soften. "Look, Dad's *obese*. He's got to *do* something about it." I heard the *tsk-tsk* of her tongue against her teeth. "I mean, how could he have let himself get that way?"

At that moment, I truly disliked my oldest daughter. Amber could eat anything she wanted without gaining a single pound. And she was beautiful, the way that my mother was beautiful— the sort of beauty who burns calories just by being there. People who saw the two of them together often thought *they* were mother and daughter, and there were times when I wondered if some bizarre cosmic mistake had occurred, presenting me with the blue-eyed, blond-haired brassy-tempered child my own mother had always wanted. Several times a year, Amber flew out to Hollywood, where she did voice-overs for commercials and received, in return, checks concluding with multiple zeros. In addition, she received alimony checks from the heartbroken British tycoon; these carried a respectable number of zeros as well. She vacationed at spas, got regular facials, had her own personal Pilates instructor. She couldn't begin to understand what it might be like for the rest of us, the world of regular people with lumpy thighs and premature crow's-feet, fast food, and morning commutes. People like, well, her father and mother.

But Jason tried to explain.

"It's not that simple," he said. "Food is both physiologically and psychologically addictive. They've done these studies with rats where they give the rats all the sugar they want and then take it away. Then they cut open their brains and—"

"No rat stories," Amber said firmly.

"Well, okay, but there's another study with rhesus monkeys—"

"No monkeys, either. The ending is always the same. Somebody cuts open their brains."

Amber was uncharacteristically sensitive when it came to nonhuman animals.

Jason sighed. "My point," he said, "is that Dad can't just go, 'Okay, I'll stop overeating now.' His whole identity—his core sense of self—revolves around food."

"Oh, I *know!*" Amber cried dramatically. "It's *disgusting*. I mean, look at this!" I heard the thump of a glass against the countertop. "This eggnog must have a kazillion calories. I want to say to him, 'Dad, can't you just give me a hug instead of feeding me? Can't we have a conversation without a ton of food between us?'"

Then why did you tell him you were parched? I was fuming. And yet I had to admit she had a point. Hadn't Harry responded to her story of Malvin's infidelity by offering her seconds?

"And look at his nicknames for us," Jason said. "Pop-Tart. Dumpling. Bacon and Egg." He was referring to the twins. "He's fixated."

Now, that was too much. Even Freud said that sometimes a cigar is just a cigar.

"He hides behind food," Amber said. "When people come over, he runs away to the kitchen. When we come home, he keeps our mouths and our stomachs full so he won't have to deal with us. It's like he's afraid or something."

"Well, he's fundamentally insecure," Jason said. "Not surprising, if you think about it. Imagine if you'd been raised by Grandma and Grampa Kligler."

We all pondered the horror until Amber said, "And then, of course, there's Mom. The other half of the problem."

What?

"If Daddy downs half a pie in one sitting, does Mom object? Of course not. She eats the other half. Then she tells him what a great pie it was. Then she asks him if he'll make another one tomorrow."

Let it be entered into the record that I have never, in my entire life, eaten half a pie in one sitting.

"If Daddy were a drinker," Amber continued, "Mom would be helping him up off the floor, saying, 'Oh, honey, don't worry about it, you just had a few too many, that's all.' "

"She's a textbook enabler," Jason said. "Dad will never lose weight if Mom doesn't stop trying to make him feel better all the time, telling him everything is fine when it isn't."

"The best thing she could do for Dad is call him a lard-ass."

"Well, that's going a bit far. Dad's a sensitive guy."

"Ever hear of tough love?" Amber's shrug was in her tone.

"You mean, like, when you leave somebody in Jamaica without a plane ticket home?"

Never eavesdrop—not because it's wrong, but because if you hear something you don't like, there is absolutely nothing you can do about it. Determined not to listen to one more word, I tiptoed up the stairs. I was breathing hard. I was sweating. I wanted to kill somebody. *He'll never lose weight if she doesn't stop trying to make him feel better.* Well, what else was I supposed to do—humiliate him, nag him, treat him the way Amber treated Malvin? How I wanted to march back down the stairs and inform my smug, ignorant children that after twenty-four years of marriage, I might know a few things about long-term relationships that they didn't, and one of those things was this: You didn't kick your partner when he or she was down. You didn't offer advice where it wasn't particularly wanted. You cast out the sort of superficial love that turned up its nose at a few extra pounds and tried to love the whole person, as you yourself hoped to be loved. It wasn't as if I was perfect. Plenty of things wiggled and jiggled when I walked—and I don't just mean the things that were supposed to. So what? We were married. We were past that kind of posturing and pretending. I knew who Harry was and he knew who I was.

I studied myself in the hallway mirror. Wide-set gray eyes. Dark, curly hair. A mouth that seemed eager to smile. *Pretty enough,* as my mother would have said. Certainly, Harry had always thought so.

Of course, I couldn't deny that—sometimes—I'd catch myself wishing Harry weren't so heavy. There were times when I had wished that we could still snuggle up together on the couch without me slipping off. Times when I worried the queen-sized bed we'd purchased only five years earlier wasn't going to be large enough. Times when I remembered the missionary position with fond affection, like a summer romance that had come and gone a long time ago, never to return. Not that I've ever been one to turn down a seat on the upper deck, so to speak. But it would have been nice, once in a while, to feel willingly overpowered, the way I had back in the days when I'd sneak into Harry's dorm room on a Sunday afternoon when everybody else was at the library. His roommate had a collection of flags from around the world pinned to the ceiling. To this day, whenever I see the Japanese flag, I think of far more than the Midnight Sun.

I wasn't angry anymore—just tired. Tired and sad and, like Jason, afraid. Harry's weight wasn't simply a matter of aesthetics anymore, and while I wasn't going to call him a lard-ass, Amber was right, in her pointy-headed way. I had to stop protecting him. I had to stop participating in his bad habits. And I had to say something to him about what I was thinking.

Now.

Harry was still awake, as I'd known he would be. He lay motionless on his back with the covers pulled up to his chin, eyes determinedly fixed on nothing.

"Hi," I said.

He didn't answer.

I changed into my nightgown, turned out all but the bedside light. "Misery loves company," I told him. "You're misery, I'm company. Move over."

He moved, but he didn't smile. "I've got to lose weight," he said.

"I know."

"I've got to go on a diet. A real diet."

"I know."

"How could I let myself go this way?"

"The kids are downstairs psychoanalyzing our relationship," I said. "Jason says I'm an *enabler*."

"Why?"

Harry's amazement made me feel better. "Because whenever you ask me if you're getting too fat, I always say you look fine."

He seemed to sink a little deeper into the mattress. "So you've been lying, is that what you're saying?"

"No," I said. *"No."* I put my head on his shoulder. "It's just that mine is not the most objective opinion in the world."

"What's that supposed to mean?" He was trying to sulk, but he wasn't very good at it.

"It means I love you," I said.

He didn't say anything.

"That was your cue to say, 'I love you, too.'"

"I was trying to think of something you hadn't heard before," he said, and then he swept me on top of him with a single practiced gesture. If memory served correctly, lying on top of a 269-pound man was considerably more comfortable than lying on top of a 169-pound man. I wondered what it would be like if Harry lost one hundred pounds. If we learned how to spend a night out together without a deep-dish pizza between us. If all the hours Harry spent cooking and I spent cleaning up were suddenly free. We'd—what? Go for long walks? Learn French? Take up landscape painting? Other than the children, what would we talk about?

Harry kissed me, and I saw that old Japanese flag begin to wave, but then I stopped it, firmly, in mid-flutter. "Promise me something first," I said.

"Uh-oh."

"A physical. As soon as possible."

"You want me to give you a physical?" He seemed to have grown an extra hand. "Turn your head and cough."

"Stop it! I'm serious."

"After the holidays." He was kissing my neck.

"As soon as Tommy Choi can see you," I said. "It isn't safe to start a diet without a physical."

He pulled back to give me a chilly look, but I hardened my heart.

"Just a minute ago, *you* told *me* you've got to go on a diet," I said. "I agree. So do the kids. We'll help you in any way we can. And the first thing I'm going to do to help is set up your appointment with Tommy."

For the first time, Harry seemed to be taking it all in. "I can't live without butter," he said. "I just want you to know that in advance."

I ignored this. "I'm sure you'll come up with all kinds of wonderful low-calorie meals."

"Not without butter."

"And you need to start thinking about what you want to do for exercise."

"Exercise," he repeated in the tone of voice a man might use to say *enema*.

"Something aerobic. Something that burns calories."

He thought about it. Then: "Sex burns calories."

"I'm serious, Harry!"

"So am I. Or do you think we should wait until after I have the physical?"

He was laughing, his breath coming warm against my ear.

"So you'll do it?" I said. My fingers were sliding across his chest; I couldn't help myself.

"Promise." He tugged my nightgown over my hips. "Now, let's get some exercise."

3

*U*nder normal circumstances, Dr. Tommy Choi was a jovial man. He was a few years younger than Harry and me, slightly built and handsome, with a taste for practical jokes. Instead of a sterile white lab coat, he wore oversized scrubs with zoo animal patterns, and he walked around in Birkenstocks regardless of the weather. The walls of his office were lined with books—not medical books, but books of poetry—and a cross-looking bust of Robert Frost sat on his desk amid the overflow of paperwork. Recently, he'd let Sue-Sue, who was now fifteen, pierce his ear, and the little gold hoop he'd selected gave him a rakish air. We'd worked together for fifteen of the sixteen years I had been at Pittsburgh Family Medical, and from time to time he and Harry had chatted at staff parties and picnics.

"It'll be easier," I promised Harry, "seeing somebody you already know."

"Just as long as it isn't that Archenbeau guy," Harry said, resigned.

Dr. Archenbeau was an orthopedic surgeon. The standing joke was that he preferred his patients unconscious. If, during an exam, a patient ventured a question, he'd bark, "No talking during exams!"

Tommy, bless his heart, had feigned delight when I told him that Harry had finally agreed to a physical during one of the busiest weeks of the year. He didn't even suggest we wait until after the holidays. "Gather ye rosebuds while ye may," he said, pulling out his prescription pad. "We better get him in before he changes his mind."

"Carpe diem," I agreed. Not for nothing had I taken a literature course in college.

Tommy laughed. "Have him drop by the lab tomorrow," he said, handing me the script. "Nothing to eat or drink after midnight. As soon as we get the results of his blood work, I'll call him in for some poking and prodding."

"I hate to think what his cholesterol might be."

"Let's be optimistic," Tommy said. "You know how it goes. Sometimes it's the three-pack-a-day guy whose lungs are clean as a whistle."

But Tommy hadn't sounded optimistic when he beeped me to say he'd heard from the lab and had scheduled Harry's physical for the end of the day—would I mind dropping by afterward? He certainly didn't look optimistic when I arrived. Even the lions and gorillas on his scrubs looked menacing. Harry, who'd already dressed, sat on the edge of the couch in Tommy's office, one of those horrible couches that threaten to swallow you whole if you lean back. The bust of Robert Frost scowled. From the hall came the sounds of people laughing and calling, "Good night!" and "Happy Holidays!" Pittsburgh Family Medical would be closed on Christmas Eve and Christmas Day. It was the afternoon of December 23. Harry had squeaked in under the wire.

"Here's the deal," Tommy said, in a voice that held no trace of humor. "Your triglycerides should be under two fifty. They're thirty-two hundred. Your good cholesterol is low and your bad cholesterol is high."

"How high is high?" I asked.

"Almost four fifty. And that's just his LDL."

"Oh," I said. Once, back in grade school, an older girl had given me a shove from behind, and I'd gotten the wind knocked out of me as I hit the ground. That was how I felt now. I tried to draw a breath, but for a moment, nothing came.

"Is that bad?" Harry said.

Tommy took off his glasses and rubbed the bridge of his nose. His eyes looked weary. "These results, coupled with your high blood pressure and your tendency to put on weight around your middle, mean you have what's called Syndrome X. Syndrome X goes hand in hand with Type II diabetes. In your case, your fasting blood sugar is extremely low."

"Well, that's good news, anyway," Harry said.

"No," Tommy said. "That's bad. You're producing way too much insulin, which is why your blood sugar levels are suppressed. But your pancreas can't keep doing this forever. Eventually it will exhaust itself—maybe in a week, maybe in six months. At that point, you'll need to start injecting insulin."

"Injecting?" Harry said. "Like, with a needle?"

The sounds from the hallway had stopped, and an otherworldly silence settled in. Even the phones had stopped ringing. We were probably the last people left in the clinic.

"Is it too late to turn things around?" I asked.

"A low-fat diet and regular exercise are essential," Tommy said, neatly sidestepping the question. "But it's one of those chicken-and-egg things. Are you hyperinsulinemic because you're obese, or are you obese because you're hyperinsulinemic?" I could see Harry flinch at each repetition of *obese*. "I won't kid you. People with Syndrome X have a tough time losing weight. You're wired to be metabolically resistant."

"Great," Harry said glumly.

"Those who succeed generally join some kind of support group. Weight Watchers, Overeaters Anonymous, that kind of thing. It's no easy thing to truly change your diet. It means changing your entire life."

I thought about Harry's neatly organized cupboards, the various sugars and candy-making supplies, the assortment of nut flours, the freezer full of prime cuts of beef, the rounds of cheese in their waxy black coats. I thought about the Sub-Zero freezer in the garage, the stacks of specialized baking pans in the attic, the clutter of cookbooks and cooking magazines in the den. It was there that he sat, night after night, surfing the Internet for hard-to-find items like foie gras and kumquats, visiting gourmet chat rooms, checking out Emeril's latest cooking tips. Mornings, he left for work before seven—taking advantage of the flex time offered by his company—just so he could be home by four, sipping wine and snacking on Saga, planning out the evening meal.

A diet would mean more than changing a few details in Harry's life. It would mean changing Harry himself.

I tried to remember what Harry had been like before he started cooking, but all I could come up with was a sweet, shy boy, his handsome face softened by what was, even back then, an extra twenty-five pounds. Someone who didn't like to be in crowds, who disliked going to parties. Someone who was happiest when it was just the two of us together, alone, in his dorm room on a Sunday afternoon. Or later, stretched out on the living room floor, Amber stomping on his hands as she toddled past, the twins propped against his stomach. Harry, the real Harry—smart, funny, surprisingly sexy—had been my special secret. Hiding behind a barbecue, a kitchen counter, a platter of hors d'oeuvres. Swaddled in a chef's apron that fell almost to his knees. Disguised beneath the extra weight so that no one could see through it, get too close.

Maybe I *was* an enabler, the way the kids had said. Maybe I'd liked having him all to myself, uncontested.

Maybe, deep down, I'd liked the fact that you had to get to know him to find him sexy.

"I can't start a diet right away," Harry said now, his voice rising defensively. "My parents are coming for Christmas dinner. I've got the ham thawing in the fridge."

"He's a gourmet cook." I heard myself pleading. "He ordered that ham from Virginia. He's had the menu planned for weeks."

"Then let that be your last supper," Tommy said. "Eat whatever you want. But *don't stuff.* I don't want to see you in the emergency room."

"And then," Harry said, turning to me, "we've got the neighborhood dinner on New Year's Day."

Tommy was unimpressed. "But won't there *always* be something?" he said. "After this dinner, there will be another, right? Or a trip. Or a party. Or a special occasion."

Harry didn't say anything. Neither did I. Tommy was speaking the truth.

"If your blood chemistries were simply off a bit, I'd say, 'Sure, whatever, start your diet after the holidays.' But you, my friend, are a ticking bomb. You need to address your weight problem *immediately,* or you may not survive another holiday season."

A little tear squeezed itself out of my left eye and traced a path down to my chin. I'd wanted Tommy to put the fear of God into Harry, but I hadn't expected him to talk like this.

"So!" Tommy said briskly; he'd noticed the little tear. "Here are my recommendations. Number one: No more than eighteen hundred calories per day. Number two: Limit your fat to twenty percent of those calories. Number three: Limit your protein to another ten or twenty percent. The rest of your calories should come from carbohydrates: fruits and vegetables, cereals, pasta. Read labels and keep a journal, tracking whatever goes into your mouth. And, of course, you need to start exercising. Your goal is four hours of aerobic exercise every week. To start, try going for a twenty-minute walk every morning. But Francie can tell you all of this, right, Fran?"

Francie *could,* it was true. But *would* she? Slowly, I shook my head. "As you can see," I said, "I'm not good at doing the bad-cop thing."

"In that case, I'll refer Harry to a nutritionist for counseling."

"That would be great," I said, just as Harry said, "Aren't there any other options?"

Tommy thought for a moment. "I've heard about a weight-loss study over at the university hospital," he told Harry. "I don't know much about it, but if you qualified, there'd be support groups, exercise programs, constant monitoring. All of it free."

"I don't have time for all that," Harry said.

"Well, these are your options," Tommy said matter-of-factly.

"Is there any diet," Harry said, "where I could still have butter?"

I stared at Harry, amazed. His very life might be at stake and all he could think about was *butter?*

But Tommy had started to laugh. He put his whole body into it—shoulders shaking, head thrown back. After a moment, I laughed, too. Even Harry smiled a little.

"Guess that's a no," he said ruefully.

HARRY AND I walked out to the parking lot. The night was clear and cold, the sound of a Salvation Army bell ringing through the air. There were only three cars left: Harry's, mine, and Tommy's.

"What am I going to do?" Harry said.

"Everything he says," I said. "You're going to eat a nice Christmas dinner, then you're going to start your diet without looking back. I'll go on it with you, okay?"

But Harry wasn't listening. "What about New Year's Day? I can't serve rabbit food."

"So we cancel the dinner. Just have drinks or something."

"*No,*" Harry said. Then, more calmly, "No. Really, I still want to have it. It's just—well, I'll have to make something separate for myself, that's all."

"For me, too," I said. "It'll be good for both of us."

But Harry shook his head. "No reason you shouldn't have a nice meal, just because I'm"—he paused—"*obese.*"

I touched his arm, expecting him to pull away, but instead he put his arms around me and we stood that way for a long time in the cold, dark parking lot. A car roared to life only forty paces away; I opened my eyes and saw Tommy's face, sympathetic, behind the wheel. I wondered how he managed to keep a reservoir of compassion for people like Harry and me. Certainly, he delivered worse news on a regular basis.

And suddenly I was thinking of my dad. He'd died before I was old enough to remember him properly, back when I was still in grade school. Like Harry, he'd been slow-moving, soft-spoken, overweight. My memories of him were like fuzzy snapshots, few and far between. A glimpse of him mowing the lawn with a cigarette dangling from his lips. A glimpse of him leaving for his law office, smelling of sweet aftershave. A glimpse of him swinging me through the air. Crawling into his lap was like clambering up a mountain. Listening to his heartbeat was like listening to a vast, echoing drum. He'd been told to go on a diet. He'd been warned that he needed to take better care of himself. And he hadn't. And he'd died. Just like that.

I hugged Harry tighter; I felt his good, warm weight. How could I have forgotten what I'd known since I was seven? We'd been lucky so far, but luck runs out. It doesn't take more than a moment for your whole life to fall apart.

"Francie?" Harry said. "Francie, it's okay."

But I held on. I was sobbing. I wouldn't let him go.

"$\mathcal{J}$f it were *me,*" Malva Miracle announced in her warm, round tones, "I wouldn't listen to some white-doctor voodoo. A body lives once, and it *knows* it lives once. That's why it's got appetites."

"He's Chinese," Harry said, pureeing Hubbard squash with freshly ground black pepper and cream.

"Korean-American, actually," I said, but nobody heard me over the noise of the food processor. When it stopped, everybody's shoulders unclenched in unison.

"A person's got two choices in this world," Malva said. "She can choose to live small, or she can choose to live large. When I die, nobody's gonna wonder which was *me.*" She held her champagne glass away from her red velvet gown and shimmied her generous hips.

No one could remember when everyone first started dressing up for Harry's New Year's Day dinner, but now it was a tradition: the women in long dresses or silk pants, the men in their best suits—all except old Mr. Polk, who wore his sergeant's dress uniform. People stood around the kitchen, drinking and getting in Harry's way, instead of migrating to the living room, where there was music on the CD player and comfortable places to sit. It always ended up like that, despite Harry's tantalizing bait: pickled jumbo shrimp on the end table; delicate rolls of salmon roe and sour cream beside the fringed parlor lamp. But Mr. Polk, with his military sense of efficiency, merely carried the plates back into the kitchen. Everybody swarmed and cooed. Now the plates were empty. The cheese platter, which hadn't even made it off the counter, was currently under attack.

"Doctors don't know squat," Malva said. "First they say you can't eat eggs. Then they change their minds. Next, salt was bad—whoops, no, salt's okay."

Harry nibbled the crackers, looked longingly at the cheese. He took a sip of his sparkling water as Mr. Polk refilled everyone else's champagne. I had tried to forgo the champagne myself, but Harry had insisted. If I wanted to diet with him, that was fine—but after the holidays. He didn't want me missing out on his account. It would only make him feel bad. Finally, I'd agreed.

Now I was regretting it.

"Then," Malva continued, "it's good-bye butter, hello margarine. Gotta eat that Day-Glo yellow stuff. Only now they're figuring out that it's full of those trans-hoosits—what do you call them?"

"Trans-fatty acids," Beth told her coolly. On the surface, she and Malva had plenty in common, forty-something black women, politically active, professionally employed. In reality, Beth disliked what she called Malva's excesses, and Malva, for her part, found Beth "cozy as an ice chip." Still, over the years, the two had developed, if not affection, at least an amused tolerance for each other. Ironically, Beth had hit it off best with Mr. Polk, who referred to her and Mari, without guile, as "ya'll lesbos."

"I like it, actually," Beth told me once. "Makes me feel, I don't know, kind of Greek."

"So now these trans—*fatty* acids," Malva continued, drawing out the word so it sounded obscene, "are holding open the door for all kinds of mischief to walk on in."

"Life," said Krys Placek. "It'll just kill you anyway, right?"

Krys was still in her early thirties, but her face wore the exhausted look of somebody much older. She had grown nearly as heavy as Harry since her second daughter was born, and the dress she wore reminded me of the muumuus my mother had favored in the seventies. Her cheeks, as always, were freckled with acne. Lately she'd developed a series of health problems—joint pain, asthma, rashes. Though I felt for her, the simple truth was that Krys was always complaining about something, and the fact that her husband, John, had just rented his own apartment and filed for divorce wasn't improving her disposition. I knew how much she must be missing John. Still, I wanted to strangle her when she raised her champagne glass and toasted the fact that life was out to get you no matter what you did.

"Like what happened with Beth's dad," Mari said, lobbing Beth a nice, soft conversational pitch.

Beth swung at it eagerly. "My dad," she said, "gets put on this blood pressure diet. No more eggs for breakfast, no more burgers for lunch. No more cheese. He's got to eat cereal and pasta and rice. And he's going out of his mind, but he does it. Well, guess what? Two months later he goes back to the doctor—"

But Mari couldn't wait for the punch line. "His blood pressure is exactly the same, but—"

"Now he's got high cholesterol to boot," Beth finished.

Harry took another sip of his sparkling water as everybody laughed. Everybody except me. What was wrong with these people? Would it have killed them to be a little bit supportive?

Malva was just being Malva, antiestablishment to the core. If a doctor had told her to breathe oxygen, she'd have found a way to photosynthesize. But Krys was always going on a diet, or planning to go on a diet, or falling off a diet. And Mari and Beth both kept in shape—Beth had a black belt in aikido, and Mari swam three times a week at the Y. And what about Mr. Polk? Certainly *he* couldn't be opposed to Harry's attempts to slim down. He'd been ribbing Harry about his weight ever since those first barbecues. *Y'all sure been out to good pasture,* he'd say, or, *Hoo, boy, I got a flat—can I borrow that spare tire?*

Harry's parents hadn't been any better—not that I'd expected any support from that quarter. On Christmas Day, when Harry mentioned he was starting a diet in the morning, Mathilde had simply shaken her head. "Diets never work," she'd assured him, holding out Harry Senior's plate for a second helping of ham and scalloped potatoes.

"That belly's genetic," Harry Senior had agreed, stabbing his fork in the direction of Harry's midsection. "Comes from your mother's side of the family."

Since retirement, Harry Senior's proportions had been catching up to his wife's, but in the interest of peace, I let it pass.

My own mother's response had been, characteristically, to the point. "Well, I should *hope* he's going on a diet," she'd said. "Unless he wants to keel over like your father did."

"I can't believe you people," I said now, trying to conceal the edge in my voice. "He's only been on his diet a few days and you're already trying to sabotage him."

"It's just that we feel guilty," Mari said apologetically. "Eating all this wonderful food when poor Harry can't even have a bite."

"There's pleasure in cooking as well as in eating," Harry said nobly.

"Bullshit," Malva said.

"One little ol' glass of champagne wouldn't hurt," said Mr. Polk.

"You could cut it with orange juice," Mari said. "It would be healthier that way."

"Not that it matters," Krys said glumly. Then, as if remembering who was boss, she glanced at me with anxious eyes. In fact, everybody did. Even Harry.

"Why are you looking at me?" I said. "I am not my husband's keeper."

But, of course, that was exactly what I'd become. I was the one who'd dragged Harry to the doctor in the first place. I was the one who'd spent the past few days pleading with him to come up with a low-fat menu, one that everybody could share. I was the one who was hovering around the cheese and cracker plate, trying not to notice that Harry, craving the cheese, had eaten the equivalent of an entire box of crackers, gourmet crackers bursting with fatty nuts and seeds. After so many years of turning a blind eye, I'd morphed into the worst kind of control freak: a passive-aggressive control freak. I was secretly documenting every scrap that slipped between Harry's lips and then, smiling brightly, trotting to the cupboard for *more* crackers so that nobody, least of all Harry, would guess how badly I wanted to shriek, "Don't eat that!"

Tonight's menu consisted of a squash soup made with port and heavy cream, followed by a goose stuffed with apricots and prunes, followed by a Gorgonzola salad with white beans. There were thick squares of basil focaccia with a special dipping oil. And for dessert: a tiramisù, which he'd labored over for hours, to be served with cappuccino and chocolate-dusted truffles.

"Why not broil us all some chicken breasts?" I'd asked, but Harry just shook his head.

"You don't understand," he said. "I don't come up with a menu that way. It's more . . . organic. I sense something. It starts to take shape. I follow it, see where it leads me."

"Okay, so you've sensed a goose and now you're hot on its heels. Can't the goose waddle past a couple of nice, lean chickens?"

Harry gave me a reproachful look. "It's more spiritual than that."

"Spiritual?"

Harry tried again. "Imagine a film director making some awful commercial when he's got this amazing idea for a documentary."

I felt as if I'd been living with an alien for the past twenty-four years.

Harry's plan was to eat a slimmed-down version of the New Year's dinner he was making. Obviously, no champagne. A small portion of goose accompanied by plain squash instead of soup. A salad stripped of the Gorgonzola. Black coffee for dessert. It had been a good plan, a fine plan, one I'd suspected would never work, even before our guests arrived to play Temptation.

The CD player had run through its selection of CDs; I went into the living room to choose a few more. Jason was supervising the Placek girls, who were sitting on the floor beside the coffee table, playing a particularly violent game on his laptop. After each explosion, they squealed and high-fived each other. They were nine and eight, and they were having a wonderful time blowing up pedestrians—something they never would have been allowed to do before their pacifistic father moved out.

"How's Dad holding up?" Jason asked, between blood-curdling screams.

"Peachy," I said, rummaging around the CD cases for what Harry called the Three Bears music: something that wasn't too hard and wasn't too soft but was exactly right. "Everybody's being terribly supportive. They're all swapping stories about failed diets."

"Like what happened to Auntie Beth's dad," Hanna Placek said, glancing up from the game.

Her sister, Ava, nodded gravely. "They put him on a diet and it just made him sick."

What was it with these people?

"This diet is different," I told her, gritting my teeth in what I hoped was a smile. "This diet is going to help Uncle Harry's heart."

There was another explosion. "Got him!" Hanna screamed. "He's toast!"

"Attagirl!" Jason encouraged her warmly. "You get extra points for decapitation." Then, to me: "Any word from Amber?"

"Nope." Amber had gone out on New Year's Eve; she still had not returned. I would have been worried except for the fact that (a) I knew she wanted me to worry, and (b) she had done this sort of thing all through high school, albeit occasionally with near-disastrous effects, and (c) I suspected she just wanted to avoid the risk of running into Malvin in our living room. He had the same standing invitation as the rest of the neighborhood "children," who would remain "children" even after they'd had children of their own. Malva, however, had made his excuses. He had spent two nights sleeping at the airport in Montego Bay, waiting for a new passport. He'd spent another twenty-four hours in customs when he finally reached the United States. Now he was catching up on lost sleep. In the morning, he had to fly to London, where he was unveiling his latest line of Miracle designs. One piece in particular—a baby crib that could be reassembled into a child's wardrobe—was already attracting plenty of interest.

Long ago, Malva and I—along with the rest of the neighborhood—had agreed to step way back from whatever madness went on between our offspring. Still, I'd expressed my deepest sympathy about the whole Jamaica incident, and Malva had accepted it.

Krys stuck her head through the doorway, stared gloomily at the carnage on the computer screen, then said something in Polish that made both girls jump to their feet. When she turned to Jason and me, I thought she was going to reproach us, too. But all she did was sigh.

"Dinner's ready," she said, scratching at the rash on her hands.

The dining room table was a vision out of a magazine: my grandmother's china, Harry's grandmother's silver, crystal water goblets we'd collected, piece by piece, since our wedding day. Out of habit, everyone headed toward their usual places like a big, noisy family, and I felt my goodwill toward all of them return, a bright, warm glow that lasted until I entered the kitchen and discovered Harry swallowing—gulping, actually—a half-glass of champagne. The last scraps of cheese, which nobody had touched for the past half hour, had vanished as well.

I had a bad feeling about that cheese.

"Hey," Harry said, too sweetly, as if the champagne glass in his hand had nothing whatsoever to do with the rest of him.

"Hey, yourself," I said coolly. "I just wanted to know if you needed help carrying stuff."

"It's all on the table but the goose," he said, lifting the serving tray. "And my diet plate. Want to carry it in for me?" He pointed to it with his chin. It held a stingy portion of goose, a mound of mashed squash, an undressed salad. The sight of it made me relent a bit. So he'd had a little champagne, some cheese. It was still significantly less than what he'd usually have eaten. Rome wasn't built in a day.

"All set?" Harry said. Then he lowered his voice. "Look, that was my first major cheat, okay?"

"Tell your confessor," I said, forcing myself to sound airily indifferent. "It's your diet, your body, not mine."

He looked relieved. "Overall, I'm doing okay," he said. "I mean, I'm really trying."

And I had to admit, he was. He carved the rich, fatty slices of goose, ladled plate after plate of stuffing, then settled down to his own lean pickings without a remorseful glance. Yes, he did have a taste of the stuffing when it became clear that nobody else was going to help themselves to the crusty scrapings left in the bowl—his favorite part. Yes, he had a few tablespoons of the sugary cranberry-lime relish he shouldn't have had, but I figured that wasn't the end of the world—at least it was fat-free. And he'd succumbed to one paper-thin slice of the tiramisù to make certain everybody's raptures weren't exaggerated. They weren't. He had another paper-thin slice, then settled back, sipping black coffee.

"To Harry," Malva said, raising her glass of dessert wine, something with overtones of apricot and peach, "who has surpassed himself once again."

Harry raised his coffee cup and everybody drank.

"To the battle of the bulge," Mr. Polk said. "May Harry lose it quick so he can eat with the gourmands again."

We all drank to that as well.

"Next year at this time," Harry said, patting his tummy, "*this* is going to be history."

He spoke with a conviction I hadn't heard before. And later that evening, as Krys helped me finish up the last of the dishes, and the rest of the gang watched football, I felt the tight knot of worry I'd carried since Christmas Eve loosen a notch or two. After all, Harry had managed to stay on his diet—for the most part—through one of the most difficult times of the year. Certainly, it would get easier. He'd develop different tastes, better habits. Weren't some of the world's best chefs on restricted diets themselves? The neighborhood would look back on this particular New Year's Day with a sense that it had been a turning point, like the day of Beth and Mari's commitment ceremony, or the births of Hanna and Ava, or the year Amber left the British business tycoon and returned to Malvin, where, even now, all of us knew she belonged. Perhaps the two of them had already reunited. Perhaps, in the morning, they'd jet off to London together, spend a few weeks holed up at a five-star Chelsea hotel. Amber's bank account, impressive though it was, was nothing compared with Malvin's. At twenty-seven, he'd already sold three of his Miracle designs to a major furniture retailer for a figure composed of many, many zeros. In addition, he created individual Miracle pieces for wealthy individuals. People like the British business tycoon, who'd fallen in love with the life-sized portrait of Amber that Malvin no longer displayed in his public studio.

As she said good-bye, Malva pulled me aside. "So where's Amber?" she asked.

I handed Malva the care package I'd made up for Malvin: goose and stuffing and tiramisù. "Actually," I said, "she was supposed to be here today, but I think she's avoiding you."

Malva snorted. "Wise girl."

"Do you think they'll make it up this time?"

Malva considered the question. "Not according to Malvin. He's had *enough,* this is *it,* he never wants to see her again." Then she grinned. "Everything he said the last time."

"Sounds just like Amber."

We exchanged rueful smiles. Whatever would happen would happen. I just hoped it would happen sooner rather than later. Our house was too small for Amber. Pittsburgh was too small for Amber.

"Well, give her my love," Malva said, enfolding me in an enormous red velvet hug. "Tell her I never took sides before, and I'm not starting now." She lowered her voice. "Even though I think she's a real piece of work."

I laughed. "Tell Malvin I'm not taking sides, either, even though I happen to agree with him this time."

Krys led the girls out shortly after that. "I was just telling Harry," she said, "that he's really inspired me. He says he needs to lose a hundred pounds?"

I nodded, surprised he would volunteer any concrete figures.

"Well, I need to lose sixty, and I've been thinking." She lifted her chin. "Starting tomorrow, I'm going to walk every morning before work. There's a two-mile loop around the cemetery. I just invited Harry to come with me."

"Won't it be awfully cold?" I said. The sprawling cemetery at the end of our street might be pretty enough by day, but winter mornings in Pittsburgh are dark, and it sounded like a creepy place to walk.

"I've got enough padding, believe me," Krys said. Abruptly, tears were shining in her eyes. Hanna and Ava studied the floor. "I've just got to do something, I'm getting so fat, and if Harry wants to do something, too . . ."

"You can help each other," I finished. I hugged her and she hugged me back. "I think it's a great idea."

Now, *this* was the sort of support I'd been hoping for. And when I went into the living room and saw Beth and Mari and Mr. Polk all drinking sugar-free lemonade with Harry instead of their usual beers, my sense of hope and possibility continued to expand until, to my own astonishment, I found myself sitting down to watch Penn State play. Harry gave me a surprised, pleased look—I had never so much as glanced at a game. (As my mother once said, "If those men would only cooperate instead of fighting with each other, they could move the ball much more efficiently.") But today I cheered and groaned along with the others, forced myself to absorb the stats Jason pulled from the NCAA Web site. When Amber finally wandered in, I found myself so genuinely caught up in the game that I hardly even managed a casual, "There you are." The two-minute warning had just sounded. Penn State and Ole Miss were tied 7–7. Ole Miss was about to punt.

"But you *hate* football, Mom," she said, clearly disappointed by my reaction—or lack of it.

"You make a better door than a window," I told her, leaning around her to see the screen. And before she could say anything more, Beth and Mari, in unison, said, "Shhh!"

I didn't often get the last word with Amber.

It had been, I decided, a perfect New Year's Day.

5

*J*t was somewhere in the wee hours of the morning when
I woke up and realized that Harry wasn't beside me.
Usually I was the nighttime prowler, the one up and down to
go to the bathroom, the one who heard noises—real or imagined—and forced herself to investigate. Tonight I was hearing
the sort of sounds I associated with Amber and the twins coming home from a date: the creak of the kitchen floor, the sticky
sound of the refrigerator opening, the muffled clank of a plate
followed by the scuff of footsteps moving into the den. Then I
remembered that the twins were in Vermont, that Amber was
sleeping off the New Year down the hall. Making a few quiet
noises of my own, I pulled on my robe and crept down the
stairs.

The kitchen was dark, but a gentle light spilled in from the
den, enough so that I could clearly see the empty platter on the
counter. The same platter that had held the remaining tiramisù—three or four servings—before we'd gone to bed. The
soup tureen, also empty, stood beside it. In the sink, soaking,
was the Tupperware container that had been stuffed with leftover slices of goose and chunks of stuffing. I poured myself a
glass of water and stared out the window into the yard, which
was cold and still in the moonlight. When I'd told Harry that I
wasn't his confessor, that it was his body, his diet, I had meant

it. But I wasn't about to stand by indifferently as he ate himself into the grave. A little tough love might be called for after all. I drank the water like medicine, took a deep breath, cinched my robe up tight. Then, feeling like a prizefighter entering the ring, I joined Harry in the den.

The den was one of those rooms we'd never decided what to do with. It had once been a one-car garage, and it still had that cool, dark, musty feeling, despite carpeting that was the color and texture of AstroTurf. When the children were small, it had served as a kind of rumpus room, but in recent years, Harry had claimed it for himself. A wall of makeshift bookshelves held his massive collection of cookbooks and cooking magazines; the overflow was stacked in various piles about the room. There was also a recliner that didn't recline, an ancient exercise bike, and a long, skinny table where Harry had set up his computer. This was where he enjoyed sitting and relaxing after supper, planning menus, jotting notes, chatting with cyberspace gourmets who boasted user names like Whiskman and Gravy-girl. This was where he was sitting now.

"Hello," he said, without looking up. He was flipping through an old *Gourmet*, studying the glossy portraits of crème brûlées and French cheeses.

I prepared to deliver a swift uppercut to the chin.

"I ate the rest of the tiramisù," he said, before I could open my mouth. "I ate the rest of the goose and stuffing, too."

It's nearly impossible to fight someone who voluntarily bares his jugular.

"I ate the leftover soup. And half a jar of peanut butter. And a big chunk of bittersweet chocolate I found in the baking cupboard."

"Oh, *Harry*." I sat down across from him, defeated. "Why?"

"I don't know," he said. "I was hungry."

"*That* hungry?"

"I wanted"—he paused—"*something*. It's hard to explain." He kept his gaze on the magazine. "I know it's disgusting."

I couldn't argue with that.

. An awkward silence fell between us. Harry continued turning page after page. "Remember this?" he finally said, sliding the magazine across the table.

The menu was titled "Romance for Two." It had been my fortieth-birthday present. Quail's eggs and caviar. London broil. Garlic soup. For dessert, a cake garnished with tiny edible flowers, which Harry had had to special-order from a nursery. He'd worn his white chef's jacket, a carnation in his lapel. I remembered how proudly he'd served me, his absolute attention to what I might need: Cracked black pepper? Another slice of beef? The pleasure he took in my pleasure. A pleasure that was sexual in its give-and-take, the way it built toward the sweet dessert, the sigh of satisfaction. And suddenly I understood. The long days of menu-planning, the careful shopping, the chopping and baking, the arranging and presenting, and, finally, the breathless compliments and growing cries of delight—these were the promises, the ear nibbles and butterfly kisses, the whispers of what was to come. To skip the meal itself after all that foreplay—well, no wonder Harry was frustrated. No wonder he crept downstairs in the darkness, burning with desire.

It wasn't just food that was killing my husband. It was food preparation itself. It was the kitchen with its copper pots, the cupboards with their labeled delicacies. It was my grand-mother's china and the warm light of the dining room, the row of eager faces, bright as candles, turning toward what-ever Harry might unveil from beneath the dome of the serving platter.

"This diet will never work," Harry said, as if he were read-ing my thoughts. "I can't cook a meal and not eat it. And I know, I *know*"—he glared at me, as if I'd tried to speak—"that I should cook low-fat meals, lots of pasta and rice and salads with nonfat dressings—"

He paused to regain his composure.

"But there's no point in cooking things I just don't like to eat. I mean, eating is one of life's great pleasures. It's the first thing you learn how to do, and when you can't enjoy it any-more, you stop, and when you stop, you die. So don't tell me to go back on my diet, Francie, because I won't. I can't."

"I agree," I said.

He was clearly surprised. "You do?"

I nodded. A plan was shaping itself in my mind. "I think you should join that alternative diet study Tommy told us about."

"That just isn't practical," he said, turning back to his mag-azine. "Where would I find the time?"

"Time won't be a problem," I said, "because from now on, I'm pulling my own weight around here."

He was listening again. "Huh?"

"You've done all our cooking and shopping for the past—what? Sixteen years? Now it's my turn. I'm taking back the kitchen. I'll shop after work. I'll cook. I'll tell you what—I'll even clean up! All you have to do is not think about food for a while. No cooking, no reading about cooking, no watching cooking shows on TV—"

"Isn't that a little extreme?"

"Think of all the extra free time you'll have—three hours a day, at least. Time to participate in a dozen diet studies."

Harry laughed then. He actually laughed. "But Francie," he said. He spoke gently, as if preparing me for bad news. "You're forgetting something. You . . . *can't* cook, sweetheart, remember?"

I was truly offended. "I can, too!"

"All right, all right," he murmured. "But I can't imagine myself involved in support groups and all that. Talking about, you know, feelings."

I couldn't imagine it, either, but I wasn't about to admit it.

"Even if it meant you didn't have to *be* on a diet?" I asked.

He stared at me. "Isn't being on a diet the point?"

I shrugged. "It depends what they're looking at. Maybe they'll manage your weight with amino acids or something. Maybe they'll be trying out some kind of fat-blocking pill."

I was lying through my teeth, but we believe what we want to believe.

"Do you think I could have butter?" Harry said.

I raised my eyebrows as if to say anything was possible.

"And, you know, I could still cook for special occasions . . ." he began, but this I nipped in the bud.

"*No.* No cooking. No clipping recipes. No foodie chat rooms. Not until you get your weight under control."

"You're *serious* about this," Harry said. It was finally sinking in. "But what will I do with myself every night?"

Exercise, I thought. Clean out the den. Sweep the garage.

Oh, yes, I could think of a few things. But I decided not to mention them right away.

"Think of it as a vacation," I said.

"A vacation!" He was still shaking his head. "What a vacation!"

But finally he agreed.

PART TWO

Insulin Insulates

6

"*I* can have butter!"

Harry burst through the front door and bounded into the kitchen, balancing an armload of paperwork and bottles of vitamin supplements. I blinked at him through stinging eyes; I'd been chopping onions. A can of beans stood waiting on the counter. Brown rice bubbled and boiled on the stove.

"Butter?" I said, sniffing back my onion tears.

Eight hours earlier, Harry had left for the university hospital with nothing but a pencil in his pocket. Lunch, the instructions said, would be provided during Orientation, as would all other necessary materials. By now, I'd been cooking for nearly two weeks, with varying degrees of unsuccess. I couldn't help but hope that the "other necessary materials" might include a supply of prepackaged low-calorie foods: foil-covered trays and microwavable pouches, diet shakes and diet bars. Perhaps this would be our last home-cooked meal à la Francie! I'd be only too happy to throw in the apron.

Butter hadn't figured into these fantasies.

"I can also have cheese," Harry said, dumping everything onto the counter. "I can even have sour cream!" He wiped an onion tear from my cheek, clucked at me sympathetically. "If you run your knife under cold water first, sweetie, it cuts the fumes."

"You told me already. It doesn't work." A quick scan of the counter revealed that there wasn't a single diet bar to be seen. "How can you lose weight eating sour cream?"

"Six to eight pounds a week for the first four weeks. Eight to ten pounds a month after that. The study lasts until the end of June, so that means—"

"Six to eight pounds a week!" Now I was concerned. "This doesn't involve surgery, does it?"

"No surgery," Harry began, but then he stopped. "Is something burning?"

The rice, of course. I spun around, grabbed for the pot just as Harry yelled, "Don't touch the—"

"Handle!" I shrieked, dropping Harry's precious Calphalon saucepan. It hit the floor and bounced with a clatter, spewing scorched rice. The cover left the scene of the crime, rolling out of the kitchen altogether. Harry already had the cold water running; I plunged my hand into the stream. A misty cloud rose from my flesh.

"Normal pots," I hissed through my teeth, "have handles you can touch."

"If you want me to start cooking again . . ."

"Oh, no," I said, swallowing hard. "I'm liking it better and better." I dried my throbbing hand. It felt larger than my head. "I don't even mind that I have to make a whole new pot of rice because, you see"—I forced a cheery little smile—"it gives me a chance to perfect the stickiness."

"But I can't eat rice anymore," Harry said. He seemed remarkably unconcerned about the pan. "Or rice cakes, either."

"Really?" Now, this was a bit of good news. We were both sick to death of rice: Minute or traditional, white or brown or wild. Since I'd taken over the cooking, we'd eaten all its incarnations, over and over again. We'd eaten mountains of pasta. We'd eaten so many salads that I feared we might turn into rabbits. "Then I'll use the beans to make a nice, uh, bean soup."

"No more beans," Harry said, holding the dustpan as I swept up the rice. "No more pasta. No more bread or crackers or potatoes." A flicker of pain crossed his face. "I'll miss the potatoes," he said to himself. "And the popcorn. I can't have popcorn, either. At least not for a while. Not until I get my blood sugar under control."

I was amazed. Popcorn was to Harry what pemmican was to polar explorers, the staple of his diet-snack cache. "What are we going to live on, then?"

"Real food for real people." He threw the burned rice into the trash and chased down the renegade cover.

I looked at him blankly. "Huh?"

"Beef," he said. "Lamb. Bacon and eggs."

"With your cholesterol?" I said.

"I'm serious," Harry said, and he pointed to the materials on the counter. "They gave us a list of the things we're allowed to eat. Basically, on this diet, you can eat all the protein and fat you want."

"We're both going to weigh three hundred pounds!"

"Fat doesn't make a person fat, Francie."

"Well, what does, then?"

"Carbohydrates!" Harry said, with all the enthusiasm of a man pulling a bouquet of flowers out of a hat. "Carbohydrates trigger the production of insulin. Insulin tells the body to store fat. What this particular diet does is limit carbohydrates so the body *burns* fat instead of storing it."

I thought about this. "I can understand not eating sugar," I said. "And simple carbohydrates like white flour. But you *need* complex carbohydrates."

"To the body, *all* carbs are sugar. It doesn't matter if they come from whole-wheat bread or oranges or rice or a candy bar." He was shaking his head. "Francie, fat isn't the culprit. It's carbs."

"But if fat is okay, then why do doctors prescribe *low*-fat diets?"

Harry laughed. "You, of all people, are not going to convince me that doctors are never wrong!"

He had a point. How many times had I come home from work with a story about a doctor somewhere who had accidentally killed somebody?

"Look, everything I learned today makes sense," Harry said. "If you stop supplying your body with carbohydrates, it will stop producing insulin. When your insulin levels come down, your weight comes down. When your weight comes down, your bad cholesterol and triglycerides will come down, too."

"How do they know it isn't the other way around?"

"Well, that's one of the things this study will be looking at. Does weight affect blood chemistries or vice versa? Which comes first, the chicken or the egg?"

"Which comes first, the stroke or the heart attack."

"*Hey,*" Harry said. "You were the one who talked me into applying for this study in the first place. And you even said that I might get to eat things like butter, remember?"

My little white lie was coming true.

"It's just—remember all the things Tommy told us? Tommy Choi isn't just any doctor, he's a friend. I feel certain he wouldn't have recommended this study if he'd known you'd be eating things like steak."

"Which reminds me," Harry said. "I think we have a couple of T-bones tucked away in the freezer."

He opened the door and began to rummage around.

"I can't believe this," I said. "You're actually going to eat a steak?"

"I am." His voice came from deep within the chilly depths. "The people who'll be in my study group? Some of them have been on low-fat diets for years. All of us are obese," he said— he could speak the word now, I noticed, without flinching— "but compared to some of them, I'm practically *thin*. Ah!" He held up the T-bones triumphantly. "Want one?"

I hesitated. I'd been planning to eat the beans as a mark of my own virtue, but instead I found my head was bobbing up and down.

"Attagirl," Harry said. "We both have to forget everything we thought we knew about dieting." He tipped the can of beans into the garbage disposal; I wasn't sorry to see them go. "And we also have to do some serious grocery shopping. All that fat-free stuff you bought? The rice cakes and fat-free cookies? On this diet, I can't eat any of it."

I shuffled through the information on the counter. There were papers on the benefits of organic produce and meats, the effects of exercise on metabolism, the function of hormones in the body. There were diagrams of the pancreas and a multicolored chart called "The Insulin Response." There were bottles of supplements Harry would be taking to help lower his bad cholesterol: evening primrose oil, borage, garlic. At the bottom of everything lay a paperback book.

Dr. Atkins' New Diet Revolution.

"They're putting you on the Atkins diet?" I tried to remember what I'd heard about it.

"Most low-carb diets draw on his research. You know, Protein Power, Sugar Busters!, Carbohydrate Addict's . . ."

I nodded as if I knew what he was talking about.

I studied the author photo on the jacket. Dr. Atkins was a sweet-looking man with white hair, a kindly grandfather whose smile invited you to enjoy that breakfast sausage, to relish that lamb chop. I flipped the book open to the recipes at the back. My eye landed on a soup that called for one avocado, two cups of heavy cream, and eight slices of bacon.

I shuddered; I couldn't help it.

"Look," Harry said, "I know this all sounds pretty weird. It did to me, too, at first. Most of what we did today was listen to Lucy talk about this stuff."

"Who's Lucy?"

"She'll be running my support group."

"What's she like?"

"She's okay," Harry said, which meant she was good-looking.

"No," I said, "what I mean is, is she helpful? Does she seem to know what she's talking about?"

"I guess," Harry said. "It's kind of too early to tell." Then he sighed. "Gosh, Francie, I'm going to be busy. Starting next week, I'll have Group every Thursday. Then Mondays, Wednesdays, and Fridays I've got to go to the gym. They gave us a choice between Tae-Bo classes or"—he rolled his eyes—"Modern Dance."

"I take it you're boxing and not dancing?"

Harry didn't deign to answer the question. "The classes run from seven until eight-fifteen. If I'm home by nine, I'll be lucky. You won't be seeing much of me for the next six months."

"All for the cause," I said.

"I could lose seventy pounds by our anniversary."

June 25 would be our twenty-fifth. We were both taking two weeks off work to travel—we still hadn't decided where.

"You'll be skinny!"

"Skinnier, anyway."

"Wow," I said, imagining Harry seventy pounds lighter. He looked terrific.

The microwave beeped, and he pulled out the steaks, dropped them onto a plate. "Now for the butter," he said, dislodging a stick from the back of the freezer. He was hacking away at it before I realized what he was doing. He was *cooking*. And I was sitting there watching him, keeping him company, just like the old days. For a moment, I was tempted to pretend that I hadn't noticed. So what if he wanted to cook one little meal? It would make him happy. It would give my burns a chance to heal. But no. In my mind's ear, I heard Jason enunciating the word *enabler*. Even Harry had agreed that a vacation from the kitchen—and old habits—was in order. A couple of innocent steaks today might lead to homemade dinner rolls tomorrow. Next thing you knew, there'd be a chocolate praline cake cooling on the counter.

"Hold it, mister!" I said, grabbing the broom and advancing on him. "Get away from that stove."

He looked sheepish. Caught! "Aw, Francie."

"Step back, nice and easy. Hands where I can see 'em."

"It's just—don't overcook them, okay? Heat the butter until it's frothy, then skim off the froth—"

I poked him in the tummy with the broom handle. "Out. I'll call you when it's ready."

Even *I* know how to panfry a steak, and I set about it eagerly. How glorious to inhale the odor of melting butter, to hear the melodic sizzle and spat of cooking beef. I flipped the steaks, bathing them in their own juices. I sprinkled them lightly with salt. I was even inspired to crush a clove of garlic, using Harry's marble mortar and pestle. Perhaps there really was a kind of Zen element to this cooking thing. Briefly, I felt I was experiencing what it was that Harry felt when he knew that a meal was going to be perfect, when he carried it to the table with shining eyes.

We fell on those T-bones as if we'd been starving, rolling our eyes to heaven. There was no conversation. There was no need. We ate and paused and ate again. At last we leaned back in our chairs. Harry studied me with fresh appreciation.

"Francie," he said. "Those steaks were just perfect."

I glowed as if he'd told me I was the most beautiful creature he'd ever seen.

He reached across the table and took my hand, kissed my palm in exactly the place I love to be kissed. But just as I leaned toward him, footsteps thudded across the front porch. Harry jerked his hand away. You can take the boy out of the Catholic Church, but you can't take the Church out of the boy.

"Amber!" he said guiltily. "I didn't hear the Mercedes."

"Damn German engineering," I said, glancing from our bloody plates to the spattered stove. "What are we going to do? The kids are going to know what we've been eating."

"Wait," Harry said. Abruptly, he started to laugh. "This is what I'm *supposed* to be eating, remember? We haven't done anything wrong."

But Amber, throwing open the door, didn't wait for explanations. She looked at the table, sniffed the air, and that was that.

"Mom!" she cried, flinging off her scarf. "How *could* you? Are you trying to *kill* him or something?"

"It's okay," Harry began, but Jason, coming in behind his sister, took up where she had left off.

"Dad! I thought you started on the study today! Didn't you go to your orientation?"

"Yes, but—" Harry tried again.

"At least you should give it a chance, don't you think? I mean—"

"You've *got* to lose weight, Daddy," Amber was pleading. "You owe it to yourself not to give up."

"You owe it to *us*," Jason said. "We love you, Dad. We want you to live a long, long time, and that won't happen if you don't stick to your diet."

Harry and I exchanged glances.

"Kids," I said. "Listen closely. This *is* your father's diet."

*   *   *

SHIFTING FROM A low-fat, high-carb diet to a diet rich in protein and fat and low in carbohydrates is kind of like becoming a Buddhist after years of Sunday-morning Christianity: You have an awful lot of explaining to do. That evening, Harry and I sat down with Amber and Jason, and together, we combed through all the materials Harry had brought home from the hospital. Even Harry had to laugh when Amber read out loud from the list of recommended snacks: macadamia nuts, deviled eggs, pork rinds. The idea of encouraging *anyone,* much less a man as heavy as Harry, to snack on pork rinds would take some getting used to.

"Everything seems well-documented," Jason said. He was poring over a complicated enzymatic study.

"Look at this," Amber said, flipping through a folder

labeled RESOURCES. "Low-carb Web sites. Low-carb bed-and-breakfasts. There are even low-carb cruises. You can spend a week in the Caribbean, Dad, did you see? With cooking classes and everything."

She held out the brochure. People of all sizes were lying by a swimming pool, waving spicy chicken wings, the bright blue ocean beyond. *The Czarina Welcomes You! Join Us for a Week of Low-Carb Luxury!*

"Looks like fun," Harry said. He was engrossed in a series of testimonials: people who had learned to manage not only their weight, but also diabetes, even heart disease, by emphasizing protein and reducing carbohydrates. A line of poetry Tommy sometimes quoted popped into my head.

Hope is the thing with feathers / That perches in the soul.

Three days later, the thing with feathers began to sing. Harry had been told not to weigh himself during his initial seventy-two hours on the study. During that time, he'd eaten less than twenty grams of carbohydrates per day, washed down with two liters of bottled water and vitamin supplements. He'd breakfasted on bacon and eggs; lunched on cheeseburgers, sans bun; dined on T-bone steaks. Hardly the sort of fare you'd think would trigger the body's fat-burning system. And yet when he awakened on the morning of the third day—

"Congratulations, big guy," cooed the scale.

I sat up in bed.

"Down seven pounds," Harry said, coming out of the bathroom.

We looked at each other and grinned.

"I think I know how Galileo felt when he realized Earth revolved around the Sun."

The kids were just as excited as we were. To celebrate, we all walked down the hill and across the highway to the shopping plaza, where there was a grocery store, a video store, a bank, and an Eat and Park. An Eat and Park, if you haven't had the pleasure, is the sort of place where the waitress greets you by saying, "Buffet?"

"Buffet," we all agreed.

Harry looked longingly at the biscuits but was soon distracted by the breakfast sausage, the ham, the bacon, the cheese steak, and the scrambled eggs. Amber filled her plate with the same. Lots of Hollywood people, she informed us, were going on high-protein, low-carb diets. Even Oprah had tried one. And didn't she look terrific?

"Maybe I should eat low-carb, too," Jason said, trying to pinch a quarter-inch of extra flesh at his waistline—and failing.

"Don't you dare," I said, forking a biscuit onto his plate.

My own plate was still empty. What was I supposed to be eating? As I circled the buffet table, every neuron in my brain was telling me that a healthy breakfast meant dry toast and orange juice, or maybe some oatmeal with skim milk—certainly *not* bacon and eggs. Eggs. Now, there was a thought. Eggs were okay by anybody's standards, as long as you didn't eat too many. I took a small scoopful of scrambled. I skipped the biscuits and breakfast potatoes, the blueberry muffins and crullers, and selected, instead, a piece of rye toast. Complex carbohydrates, rather than simple. According to Harry's information, they contained more fiber, which offsets carbs to a certain extent. But what to put on my toast? Jelly was sugar, and besides, who wants jelly on rye? Butter was fat, and not just any old fat, but animal fat. Animal fat was bad. Only Harry was eating loads of animal fat, and he'd just lost seven pounds.

What to do. I took a pat of butter. I also took a sausage

patty—but just one, because I felt guilty. Then I turned to the fruit. What could be better than fruit? Grapes, watermelon, pineapple. Yet wasn't fruit just sugar dressed up for a party? I eyed the strawberries. Strawberries were low in sugar. Even Harry could eat strawberries. But I was fairly certain that the Eat and Park didn't stock organic strawberries, and one of the more disturbing studies Harry had shown me demonstrated that strawberries absorb a truly obscene amount of pesticides. Washing them didn't help. *If you buy only one organic item at the market,* the report concluded, *make it strawberries.* I nixed the strawberries. Instead, I grabbed the plastic tongs and ferried a few slices of kiwi onto my plate. I'd never heard a word against kiwi before. Kiwi, scrambled eggs, rye toast, sausage.

It looked weird. I ditched the sausage.

It still looked weird.

"What's the matter, Mom?" Jason called from the table. "I've got to be at school in half an hour." He and Amber and Harry were hunkered down over their plates, shoveling away like truckers.

"I don't know what I should eat anymore," I said.

"Pork rinds," Amber said through a mouthful of bacon.

I thought of Krys Placek on New Year's Day, toasting the fact that life would get you no matter what you did. Maybe she had a point.

I loaded my plate with sausage.

7

"Well, I don't think anybody should eat pork rinds," Tommy said, sitting down across from me in the staff room table and kicking off his Birkenstocks. "But I've heard some intriguing things about these low-carb diets. How much weight has Harry lost?"

It had been nearly three weeks since Harry joined the university study. I wasn't sure whether to be frightened or elated.

"Sixteen pounds," I said.

"Whew!" Tommy whistled.

"Is it dangerous?"

He bit into his apple, chewed reflectively. "Not as dangerous as obesity," he said. "As long as his kidneys are healthy and he keeps himself hydrated, he should be okay." He paused, gave me a frank look of assessment. "You've lost some weight yourself, haven't you?"

I nodded, pleased. "Basically, I'm just staying away from sugar and flour."

"Well, you look terrific."

"I *feel* terrific. Must be all the butter."

Lunch was officially over, but here we were in the staff room, just opening our paper bags. I'd been delayed by a pediatrics case—a hyperflexible seven-year-old who kept dislocating his thumb on purpose—and Tommy by a highly peculiar situation involving a man with a colostomy bag who'd swallowed half a dozen marbles.

"He kept saying, 'Don't ask,' so I didn't," Tommy said. "Nasty infection, poor devil. Took quite a while to flush everything out."

"Nearly a full moon," I observed, still thinking about the seven-year-old. He'd dislocated his thumb so many times that I'd needed to splint the hand to protect the ligaments. I'd spent a long time explaining why he should never dislocate it ever again, even when the kids at school begged him to, did he understand? He'd nodded solemnly. But as soon as the splint was dry, he'd dropped onto his stomach, hoisted his feet up over his shoulders so that his body formed an O, and crab-walked across the cast room floor. "Isn't he amazing?" his mother squealed. "We're trying to get him on *Ripley's Believe It or Not.*"

I wondered how long it would be before I was trying to splint his hips.

"Full moon," Tommy echoed, finishing his apple. "Funny, I just read something interesting about that. Anthropologists surveyed two thousand medical professionals about the effects of the full moon, and we overwhelmingly agreed that more babies were born, that there were more odd cases, that kind of thing. But when these anthropologists compared our responses to actual hospital medical records, they discovered there was no difference. In fact, birth rates were a little bit lower around the time of the full moon."

"Facts don't always tell the truth." I'd finished the last of my chicken salad, and now I turned to my sliced avocado, ignoring the little calorie-counting voice inside my head that was shrieking, *How can you eat an avocado after all that fatty mayonnaise?!*

Old habits die hard.

"I hear you," Tommy said. "But my point is this. Ask people how to go about losing weight, and they'll say reduce calories, reduce fat, that kind of thing. I say it myself; it's what I've been taught. But studies like the one Harry's part of could very well show that popular belief runs contrary to fact. I can't wait to repeat his blood work, if he ever comes back to see me."

"He will," I said, though I doubted it.

"I was doing my bad-cop routine, as I recall."

"You certainly were."

"Sorry."

"No, he needed to hear it. *We* needed to hear it."

"All these diets," Tommy mused. "All these theories. But if you really think about it, they all boil down to the same old-fashioned advice: Go for whole foods. Stay away from processed stuff. It's like my mother use to say: Eat a little bit of everything. And take small bites so that, if you don't like it, you can spit it into your napkin without anybody noticing." He took aim with his apple core, then hooked it into the trash can by the window. "Jessica's on this diet where you divide your plate into thirds. Thirty percent protein, thirty percent fat, forty percent carbohydrates."

"Protein Power," I said. "See, I'm an expert on all these diets now. But why is Jessica trying to lose weight? She's perfect as she is."

For some reason, acknowledging this made me blush. Jessica was Tommy's wife. I'd gotten to know her a bit during the months I'd worked on Sue-Sue's ankle. Since then, I'd seen her once or twice a year, at office parties. She was built exactly like Tommy, only slinkier. And blond.

"She's decided to trim the excess from her life," he said. "That means shucking five pounds and giving up coffee and getting rid of me."

I thought I'd misheard him, but then I saw I hadn't.

"Aw, Tommy, I'm sorry."

He shrugged, but his smile wobbled a bit. "She rented a condo, and I helped her move in. She cooked me a wonderful dinner to thank me. Then she sent me home."

"So things are civilized at least?"

He nodded. "I keep hoping that a little time, a little space . . . well, you know."

"Where's Sue-Sue?" I asked.

"With her mother." For the first time, Tommy lost his smile completely. Then he brightened again. "But she's coming home for the weekend. She says she misses our house."

"That's teen-speak for missing her dad," I assured him.

"'Tell all the Truth, but tell it slant,'" he quoted. "Do you think Emily Dickinson was writing about fifteen-year-old girls?"

"I have no doubt whatsoever," I said.

"I forgot you've been through this."

"Three times. And survived it."

Tommy's beeper went off. He checked it, then stepped back into his Birkenstocks.

"Sorry to eat and run," he said, "but it looks like I may have missed a marble."

After he'd gone, I sat for a while, trying to collect my thoughts. Jessica and Tommy had been married nearly as long as Harry and me. On the surface, at least, they'd always seemed perfectly happy. Tommy, the jolly extrovert; Jessica, elegant and reserved. Opposites, the way so many couples were. Certainly Harry and I seemed to balance each other out in a similar way. Harry was the quiet type; I was the talker, the emotional one. Harry balanced the checkbook; I wrote the thank-you notes. Harry drove; I studied the map, pointed us both in the right direction. We were a team, the way Tommy and Jessica had been a team.

Only now they were separated.

I tossed what was left of my avocado into the trash. I wasn't hungry anymore. It was deeply upsetting to hear about a couple like that breaking up.

*   *   *

VALENTINE'S DAY HAPPENED to coincide with the full moon. Any anthropologist who believes that the moon has no effect on human behavior is hereby invited to Pittsburgh Family Medical. First thing in the morning, a man walked into our waiting room, smiled, and pulled down his pants to reveal some highly original tattoos. " 'Nature red in tooth and claw,' " Tommy observed as the police carted him away. Shortly thereafter, a woman—one of the witnesses—went into cardiac arrest. And then, in the afternoon, an elderly gentleman we all knew and loved came in for a checkup. He'd been feeling a little bit tired. He asked to use the rest room and never came back out. We knocked, we listened, we got the key and entered. Yes, he had died—quite peacefully, it appeared. But Tommy took it hard. Recently, he'd been taking everything hard. By now, everyone knew that Jessica had left him.

"This day," he muttered, gulping paper cups of water from the cooler, "reminds me of that Chinese curse: May you live in interesting times."

Fortunately for me, Valentine's Day also happened to fall on a Tuesday—the only weeknight that Harry made it home for dinner anymore. Driving home, I realized how much I was looking forward to seeing him at the head of the table, hearing about his day and telling him about my own, curling up on the couch after dinner to find out what Seinfeld was up to. It struck me then like a physical pain: I missed my husband. I missed doing things together—running errands, cooking, puttering around the house—and I missed doing nothing together. I missed talking with him and laughing with him. I missed the luxury of sitting in silence because everything had been said.

Mondays, Wednesdays, and Fridays, Harry usually stayed at work until it was time for him to go to his Tae-Bo class. The gym, it turned out, was a block from his office. It didn't make sense for him to fight traffic home, bolt his supper, then turn around and battle his way back into the city. Several times I had met him for sashimi at a nearby Japanese restaurant, but the truth was that since he'd started dieting, I'd gotten just as busy as he was. I'd always done the lion's share of the house-work—Harry remained stubbornly unliberated on the vacuum-cleaner front—but now I was doing all the shopping and cooking as well. Things at the clinic had been particularly crazy, and I often wound up staying late, shoveling out from beneath the latest landslide of HMO paperwork. And with Amber home, well, Amber was a part-time job unto herself. She was kind of like an exotic pet: beautiful and loving, but requiring lots of attention. One minute she'd purr; the next, she'd bite. She left long hairs on the furniture. She followed me from room to room. One night, waiting for Harry to come home, I went into our bedroom and found her curled up on our bed. In her hands was the very book I'd been reading.

"Mind if I borrow this?" she said.

Thursday nights, Harry met with his support group, and then, afterward, they all went out for steaks at a nearby Outback restaurant. Even Lucy went along sometimes. Harry hoped I didn't mind about him being away from home so much.

"It's okay," I told him, and I meant it. Harry had lost more than twenty-five pounds. His blood chemistries were improving. Before my eyes, he was being transformed into a younger, more energetic version of himself. No more naps on the couch after supper. No more stifled yawns at breakfast. The dark circles beneath his eyes had faded and, as Jason pointed out, he was starting to look a lot less puffy. "As far as I'm concerned," I said, "the time you spend with your group is time well spent. I see it as an investment in our future."

Harry's arms tightened around me. We were lying in bed. We were making love, or trying to, but we kept getting distracted.

"There are people in Group whose wives are getting kind of mad about it," he said. "Husbands, too. I guess I'm pretty lucky."

"You guess?"

"I *am* lucky."

"That's better."

"I'll make it up to you in June," he promised. We were still deciding where we wanted to go for our anniversary. I was leaning toward Hawaii, but Harry thought that Paris would be more romantic. Besides, he could eat the cheese.

"I suppose it would be harder," I said, "if we still had small children at home."

I'd returned to what he'd said earlier about people's spouses getting mad. But Harry didn't need to think twice about what I meant. Automatically, effortlessly, he'd leaped after me and landed on the same page.

"You mean Amber doesn't count?"

And this was what I loved about us, about the twenty-four years that bound us thick as blood. Who cared if, sometimes, we took all our clothes off and then forgot we happened to be naked? Who cared if he was eating away from home four nights a week?

Stuck in the Squirrel Hill tunnel, inching my way toward home, I made up my mind to adjust my attitude. From now on, I'd stop mourning the time we didn't have together. Instead, I was going to make the most of the time we *did* have. And to kick off this new resolution, I was going to cook a special Valentine's Day meal. Certainly I wasn't up to the kind of feast that Harry might have prepared—something with five courses and a flaming dessert—but still. There were free-range chicken breasts in the refrigerator. There was a head of cauliflower in the crisper. Hadn't I read something in one of Harry's pamphlets about substituting cauliflower for mashed potatoes? And hadn't a new package of cheese just arrived from one of the tasting clubs whose membership Harry had forgotten to cancel? I'd serve sparkling water with twists of lime, steamed asparagus with butter. Now that I was cooking, I understood why Harry had fought so hard to keep butter in his repertoire.

Butter transformed the dull into the delectable. Butter was the difference between a cook and a chef. I remembered something my old college roommate, Lindy, had liked to say: *Anything in life worth striving for is illegal, immoral, or substrate for butter.*

Lindy hadn't lied.

As soon as I got home, I set to work. Marinating the chicken, trimming the asparagus, I felt the day's tension falling away. Harry's crazy schedule, the weekly clinic staff meeting, Tommy and Jessica, the naked and the dead—suddenly, none of it mattered. NPR was on the radio. The kitchen was warm as a cocoon. Here was the recipe; there were the measuring spoons; here was the motion of my knife. Everything simple. Everything clear. Each gesture as old as civilization itself. Even Amber and Jason, quarreling like ten-year-olds over the television remote, couldn't get under my skin. I was just pulling the chicken out of the oven when Harry walked through the door, a bouquet of yellow roses in his arms.

"Happy Valentine's Day," he said. "Hey, that smells great."

I took the flowers and kissed him. "You're just in time."

The chicken was perfectly seasoned and only slightly overdone. The cauliflower, which I'd mashed with garlic, really did taste like potatoes. Harry complimented everything, and yet he seemed distracted. Distant. The way he often was on Thursdays after coming home from Group. Clearly, these counseling sessions were leaving him with a lot on his mind. I couldn't help but wonder what he talked about with Lucy. Okay, what I really wondered was this: What did he say about me? After all, I was doing everything I could to be supportive. So were the kids. If Harry had a question about the carb content of a particular food, Jason leaped to research it online. Amber, showing uncharacteristic sensitivity, had started keeping her stash of gummy bears hidden away in her room. Trish and Tina had sent him a set of hemp sweatpants and a matching sweatshirt, hand-dyed with juniper berries, and several packs of zero-carb gum made out of slippery elm.

So then why was Harry evasive whenever I'd ask, directly, "How was Group?"

"Oh, you know," he'd say.

And I'd say, "Not really. What's it like?"

And he'd say something like, "It's not so bad."

"Not so bad?"

"It's fine."

Fine. Not so bad.

I knew a dead end when I came to one.

Tonight's conversation was a similar series of dead ends. How was work? Fine. How was traffic? Okay. More sparkling water? No, thanks.

What on earth was the matter?

Fortunately—or, perhaps, not so fortunately—Amber was more than willing to fill any awkward silences. She had heard from her agent that morning. She'd be flying out to Hollywood next week to tape a commercial promoting a kind of sports car, she couldn't remember which one. Something with capital letters in it. Possibly a Z.

"Do you get to drive the car?" Jason wanted to know.

"What I get is a trip to some recording studio. I'll never even *see* the car."

"You're buying a car?" Harry said, blinking like a man just coming to.

"Daddy! You aren't even listening to me!"

"Sorry," he said sheepishly.

"Are you all right?" I asked.

He didn't meet my eye. "Long day at work, I guess."

"Is everything okay?"

"*Yes,*" he said irritably. Then, as we all looked at him, he put his head in his hands.

"No," he admitted. "Everything's not okay."

I felt the blood leave my face. Start-ups like Harry's company were fickle. They dumped their employees without fanfare— only, of course, they didn't say "dump" or even, for that matter, "downsize." Firing someone was referred to as "encouraging the pursuit of alternative career opportunities."

Harry must have guessed what I was thinking.

"Don't worry," he said. "I'm still employed. It's just that I'm a forty-seven-year-old programmer saying 'Yes, yes, yes' to twenty-six-year-old managers and directors." He ran his hands through his hair. "The fact of the matter is, I got into this game too late. These kids cut their teeth on computers."

"So do something else," I said. "Go back to school. We'll manage."

For a moment, he seemed to consider this. Then he sighed. "Aw, Francie, the job isn't the problem. It's me." He gave me a wry smile. "It's not like any of this is breaking news. I've been saying 'Yes, yes, yes' to twenty-six-year-olds for the past five years. I don't know why it's getting to me now."

"Maybe," I said, "it's because you aren't cooking anymore." As soon as I said it, I knew it was true. "You used to leave work at work, you know? As soon as you walked in the door, you were busy in the kitchen. Now you come home and—"

"I don't know what to do with myself," Harry finished for me. "It's true."

"Maybe we could let you back into the kitchen a couple of nights a week."

But Harry shook his head. "I need to figure out what I'm good at, besides cooking and eating. I need to develop other talents. That's what they tell me in Group, anyway."

"Group?" I pricked up my ears.

"And you know what? They're right. I mean, I'm pushing fifty. Half my life is over, and I still haven't accomplished anything substantial."

"Excuse me," I said. "I'm substantial. Your four children are substantial."

"I don't mean it like that," he said quickly. "But there has to be more to life than just going to work and coming home and paying the bills and . . . I don't know. Planning the next meal. Watching the kids leave. Waiting for the next thing to happen. When I'm dying, I don't want to look back on my life and think, How *ordinary*."

He stopped then, seeing our faces.

"Sorry," he said quickly. "I'm just kind of thinking out loud. Lucy says that's what happens when you stop stuffing your face. Words come out instead of food going in."

"That's a good thing, Dad," Jason said.

"Is it?"

"Yes," I said firmly. "If something's wrong, we need to talk about it."

"But that's the thing," Harry said. "Nothing's *wrong,* exactly. It's just—" Suddenly he turned to me. "Remember Barney?"

I nodded, surprised.

"Who?" Amber said.

"A dog Daddy used to have," I explained. Barney had been a fat black lab. He'd died shortly after we started dating. Frankly, it had been a mercy.

"Every Saturday," Harry said, "when I was a kid? My mother would wash Barney's bed and dry it outside on the line. The whole time, Barney would pace and whine and pace because he didn't know where he was supposed to be. Ever since I stopped cooking, that's what I've been feeling like."

I didn't know what to say.

"It's a Tuesday night. I always made bread on Tuesdays. I'd be sitting in the den right now, pulling down my bread books, trying to decide between walnut raisin or a nice rosemary olive. Remember how we'd split the heel?" he asked Jason. "You and me. We'd eat it straight out of the oven."

Jason considered this. "Sure, I remember," he said. "But to tell you the truth, I never liked the heel that much."

Harry stared at him. "You didn't?"

"I just liked it because you liked it."

"I always thought you liked it."

An awkward little silence settled around the table. Harry wiped his mouth on his napkin, then pushed back his chair.

"There's dessert," I said. "Portuguese cheese with walnuts and pears."

But Harry shook his head. "Thanks, but I'm not hungry," he said. "I was thinking I'd go for a little walk."

"It's ten degrees out," I said, surprised.

He was already bundling up in his coat. "I won't be long. I'll help with the dishes when I get back, okay?" He wrapped an old black-and-white-striped scarf around his head and headed for the door. The skunk scarf, the kids had always called it. It belonged to no one and everyone. It had been in the family for such a long time that none of us could remember where it had come from.

"Do either of you want dessert?" I asked the kids, without enthusiasm.

Without enthusiasm, they shook their heads.

"Not really," Amber said.

"I've got homework," Jason said.

All of us, it seemed, had lost our appetites.

I got up and walked to the front window. Harry was crossing the lawn toward the sidewalk; I could see the white stripe of the skunk scarf, glowing in the moonlight. When I lay dying and looked back on my life, I was pretty sure that I'd see lots of details like the skunk scarf. I'd remember the private jokes, the family eccentricities, the Christmas clock. And I wouldn't feel I'd been ordinary. I would feel that I'd been a part of something wonderful and complete.

I knew that, deep down, Harry felt the same way.

Amber had already started on the dishes, attacking the broiler pan with a zeal I found disturbing. As her time away from Malvin increased, so did her restlessness, and this restlessness was expressed by compulsive fits of cleaning. It was a cycle I'd charted before; once again, I was recognizing symptoms. The silver in the drawer had been polished. The tile in the upstairs bathroom gleamed. The smell of lemon Pledge drifted out from under her bedroom door.

"Let me do that," I began, but she fixed me with a look.

"Mom," she said. "You don't get things clean. This pan is truly disgusting."

"It's seasoned."

"It's rancid!"

Seasoned or rancid. Ordinary or comfortable. There was no point in arguing about such things. They were each in the eye of the beholder.

"Fine," I told her. "You want the dishes? You've got the dishes."

"You're welcome," Amber said.

Now *I* was feeling like Barney. Restless, I wandered into the den and climbed up onto the exercise bike, where I pedaled slowly, lethargically, until the chain slipped off the wheel. Suddenly I felt completely overwhelmed. We needed to get a new exercise bike. We needed to clean out this pit of a den. We needed to get the furnace serviced. The laundry was piling up again. . . .

Then I realized what was happening.

Stop it, I told myself firmly. I was catching Harry's mood like a bad case of flu. The only way to ward off the disease was to treat the symptoms aggressively. Laughter is not only the best medicine, it's also the least expensive, and you don't need to drive to the pharmacy to get it. I hurried upstairs to our bedroom, grabbed the phone off the night stand, and dialed my old roommate, Lindy.

The phone rang and rang, but I was patient. Lindy, being Lindy, wouldn't even notice the phone until it had been ringing for quite some time, and then she would have to locate the phone, which would require another fifteen rings, minimum. Lindy's life had been turned upside down when, at forty-four, she'd given birth to her first and only child. Raymond was the spitting image of Lindy's husband, Max. He had round blue eyes and bright red curls and a smile that could charm the rust off a nail. He was also—like Max—astonishingly hyperactive. Only Max, of course, was an adult. He'd had nearly fifty years to discover constructive outlets for his boundless energy. He was a trial lawyer. He ran marathons. In his spare time, he practiced what he called extreme sports: skydiving, ice climbing, bungee jumping. No doubt, Raymond was destined to follow in his father's footsteps. But Raymond was only three years old. It was illegal, in the state of Pennsylvania, to enroll a three-year-old in bungee-jumping classes.

At last somebody picked up the phone—or, rather, knocked it off the hook.

"Just a minute!" Lindy's voice seemed to come from the bottom of a well. There was scuffling and a loud bang, followed by a demonic giggle. Finally I heard Lindy's breathless "Hello?"

I considered launching into a pitch for long-distance phone service—but no. I wasn't that cruel.

"Hey, Lindo," I said.

"Oh, God," Lindy said.

"Close. It's Francie. What's the matter?"

"I'm flying solo with Raymond all week while Max is away on this skiing trip."

"And you were of sound mind and body when you agreed to this?"

"In exchange, I get a week at the beach this summer."

"Separate vacations?"

"You take what you can get."

"Well, I guess it's a fair trade."

"No, it's not," Lindy said. "Because, you see, I am not going to make it through this week. By the time my week rolls around—wait—oh, Christ. BACK INTO THE LAUNDRY ROOM! EVERYTHING OFF! SOCKS, TOO!"

I waited for the ringing in my ear to subside. "What did he get into this time?"

Lindy made a helpless sound. "I left him watching a video for, what? Three minutes? By the time I come back, he's throwing up. We're talking Mount Vesuvius here. So I say, 'My goodness, Raymond, what happened?' And he says, 'I stuck my fingers down my throat.' "

"Why did he do that?"

"A fair question. The same question, in fact, that I asked."

"And the answer?"

"He just wanted to know what was down there."

Lindy laughed in spite of herself, and I laughed, too. Then there was a crash in the background.

"PUT THE SCISSORS DOWN, RAYMOND. WE DON'T PLAY WITH SCISSORS."

"You know what?" I said. "I think I've caught you at a bad time."

"Is there any other kind?"

"Hang in there. Max'll be back soon."

"Not soon enough. Hey, I'm sorry—how are *you* doing? You sound a little down."

"I'm fine."

"How's Harry's diet? RAYMOND, NO! I've really got to go, okay? Love you."

"Love you, too."

The line went dead.

I lay back on the bed. This, I confess, was not the kind of medicine I'd had in mind. In fact, it was more like being exposed to a second, more virulent disease. Now I not only felt down, I was also feeling *guilty* about feeling down. After all, what was a mildly confused husband against a vomiting three-year-old with scissors? So Harry was a little bit bored. Well, who wasn't? It was February. It was freezing. We hadn't seen the sun in nearly a week. All the more reason, I thought, to choose a warm and sunny destination for our anniversary. June in Paris might be romantic, but it wouldn't be any warmer than June in Pittsburgh. Hawaii, on the other hand, would be hot and steamy. Both of us, I thought, could use a little heat and steam. Harry's schedule—not to mention his mood—hadn't done much for the chemistry between us.

The phone rang; I snatched at it eagerly. Had Lindy been reprieved?

But no. It was my mother.

"You sound awful," she said, matter-of-factly. "What's wrong?"

Even as a child, I never could tell her anything but the truth. "Harry's in a mood," I said.

"Full moon," my mother said.

My mother and I—to tell another truth—have never been what you'd call *close*. Yet at moments like this, I adored her. And I knew she adored me in turn. How else would she have known the perfect thing to say?

"Don't hold it against him," my mother said. "He can't help himself. All men are part werewolf, didn't you know that?" She laughed wickedly. "Of course, some have bigger parts than others." Sexual innuendo was my mother's favorite pastime. She'd wedge it into a conversation with a crowbar if she had to. "But it's the size of the howl in the wolf, right?"

She gave a long, low wolf whistle.

"Where did you learn to do that?" I said.

"An investment banker taught me. I met him on the golf course."

"What happened to the horse breeder?"

"Once he explained the procedure, I could never stop wondering if he'd washed his hands."

"Don't *ever* tell me the procedure."

"Not to worry. You'd like the investment banker better, anyway. The only thing he dirties his hands with is money. Plus he has a full head of hair."

"Sounds dreamy."

"So how's Harry's diet?"

"Fine," I said. "Better than fine. He looks terrific."

"Speaking of dreamy," my mother said, "I always *thought* he'd be a looker if he lost about ten of those chins."

My mother's tact never ceased to amaze me. "He always looked good to me, Mom," I said.

"Well, he's going to look good to anything with a pulse if he shucks a hundred pounds."

"He's lost twenty-five."

"How exciting! Let me say hello to the man."

"He went for a walk."

"At eight o'clock in the evening? In subzero weather?"

"I told you. He's in a mood."

"Male menopause," my mother said.

"You just said it was the full moon!"

My mother's shrug was in her tone. "Beats me why men do what they do. It's like Gloria Steinem says: Stay away from strange men, and remember all men are strange as hell."

"Gloria Steinem never said that!"

"Maybe it was Margaret Thatcher then."

I was laughing when I heard the front door slam.

"Mom," I said, "I have to go."

"He's back, is he?"

"Uh-huh." Now I could hear footsteps on the stairs.

"Gonna kiss and make up?"

"Hope so."

"Have fun. Tell Amber to give her old Grandma Sylvia a call."

Amber was my mother's unabashed favorite.

"Who was that?" Harry said, coming into the room. He sounded like his usual self.

"Mom," I said. "She says hello."

"How's the horse breeder?"

"Replaced by an investment banker."

"Go, Sylvia," Harry said. He sat down on the edge of the bed. I noticed he was holding something in his hand, keeping it just out of sight. "Sorry about before," he said. "I spoiled a really nice dinner."

"Do you want to talk about it?"

"Actually, I'm feeling better. I've made up my mind about something."

"Oh, yeah?"

"I had an idea."

"About our anniversary trip?" I said. "Funny, I was thinking about that, too."

Harry looked surprised. "Actually," he said, "I was thinking about work."

"Oh," I said.

"This idea—if I'm right? It could really streamline the software package we've been trying to put together. I was thinking I'd schedule a cluster bluster and make a formal presentation."

A cluster bluster, I remembered, meant a board meeting.

"The thing is, I've had some good ideas before," Harry said. "Great ideas, in fact. But I always hold back. I'm afraid I might have missed something. I'm afraid of making a fool of myself. Then, next thing I know, somebody else ends up suggesting the same thing."

"Well, it sounds like this time will be different," I said.

"I want to take some *risks*." He fell back beside me on the pillows. "I want to challenge myself!" Suddenly he laughed. "Am I scaring you yet?"

"A little," I admitted. "But I think it's exciting, too."

He rolled over to face me. "Here. I brought you something."

"What is it?"

I felt something cold pressed into my hand. A pinecone. I held it to my nose, breathed in the rich scent of pine. "I don't know," I said. "It's awfully ordinary."

"It's lovely," Harry said firmly. "Like you."

He took the pinecone and trailed its smooth tip over my cheek.

"Promise me something," I said.

"Anything."

"Whenever you feel like Barney and you don't know where you're supposed to be? Just ask me."

"Okay."

"Because I'll always know the answer. You're supposed to be with me."

That night, we did make love—carefully, attentively, looking into each other's eyes as if it were our first time. In the shadowy light from the window, I saw his changing body. I ran my hands over newly emerging collarbones and ribs. It was almost like being in bed with a stranger. It was almost like having an affair.

8

*M*arch came in like a lion. April came in like a lion, too. This was, after all, Pittsburgh.

In the midst of all the snow and dark and cold, Jason found a girlfriend. I hadn't met the young lady in person, but I felt as if I'd known her for years. At any rate, her name seemed to crop up every time Jason spoke. "I'm going to the library with Mary Elizabeth," he'd say. Or "I'm going to study at Mary Elizabeth's house." Mary Elizabeth had applied to Stanford and MIT, just like Jason. Mary Elizabeth was also planning to go for her M.D., only Mary Elizabeth was into biotech, genetic alterations, that kind of thing.

So when were we going to meet Mary Elizabeth?

"Anytime," Jason said. "Just let me know when you and Dad will both be home."

This was easier said than done. The good news was that Harry's idea had been a wild success at the cluster bluster. Two weeks later, after a second, private meeting with the CEO, Harry was given a "catapult" (i.e., a promotion). Now he was a project manager, with a budget all his own. The bad news was this: If I'd thought he'd put in long hours before, that was nothing compared with his new schedule. There were nights he headed back to work for an hour *after* he'd gone to the gym; there were weekends when he worked all day Saturday, plus a few hours Sunday afternoon. He and his team were "architect-ing software," which, based on Harry's idea, would "revolu-tionize B2B relationships." The software still was "vaporware," which meant it wasn't actually in existence. But the marketing team was already pitching the concept. In the meantime, Harry had hired some "code monkeys" so he and his team could focus their attention on "the bigger picture."

I nodded as if I understood what the heck he was talking about.

"You know what, Francie? I love being a manager. I love get-ting people together, working as a team."

"That's great," I said. "I just wish you didn't have to work such crazy hours."

"If the IPO happens, it's going to be worth it. We could all be living on a yacht somewhere."

"I don't want to live on a yacht with Amber."

"We're going to be rich, remember?" Harry said. "We'll buy her a yacht of her own."

At least he wasn't feeling like Barney anymore. He had found a new blanket, a niche all his own, and I was pleased to see that, for each pound of flesh lost, an added ounce of confi-dence appeared. But I hated the fact that he was gone so much of the time. I hated the late meals, the rushed conversations. I hated feeling as if our relationship had been put on hold until *after:* after the diet study, after the IPO, after Amber moved out of the house. When I'd imagined Harry losing weight, I hadn't anticipated other losses, too.

Evidently, I was not the only spouse who felt this way. Early in April, I received a letter inviting me to a Saturday "Spouse Grouse" at the hospital. It would be a time for "diet widows

and widowers" to "share experiences and express concerns."
We were urged to bring our collective sense of humor. Lunch—
low-carb, of course—would be served.

"Lucy's going to be running it," Harry said when I told him
about the letter.

So I'd finally get to meet the famous Lucy!

I couldn't wait.

*   *   *

THE MORNING OF the Spouse Grouse, I awoke before dawn
to the chatter of the New You Digital Scale. By now it had
"learned" a great deal, just the way Jason had promised.

"Two hundred and twenty-one pounds of Grade A prime
U.S. government beefcake!"

I sat up in bed and turned on the light. As far as I was concerned, that scale had learned a little too much.

"You hear that?" Harry said, coming into the bedroom.
"Almost fifty pounds. And Krys has lost twenty, did I tell you?
All she did was stop eating pasta and bread. Plus that weird rash
she used to have is gone. She thinks she was allergic to wheat."

Krys and Harry had been walking together Tuesday and
Saturday mornings. I'd gone with them a couple of times, but
the cold and the dark, coupled with the gravestones, hadn't left
me eager to sacrifice the extra forty minutes of sleep.

"Good for her," I said. "And good for you."

"Thanks. Say hi to Lucy for me."

I listened to him whistling his way down the stairs. After
walking with Krys, he'd head straight to the office, where he'd
spend the rest of the day with his team. They were working with
Marketing now, finalizing financial projections. The code mon-

keys had finished up the "beta version" of the software, and now a couple of "major VCs" wanted in.

"Vietcong?" I'd asked.

"Venture capitalists."

I showered and dressed, and half an hour later, I was following the smell of bacon and eggs into the kitchen. The odor brought back the good old days when Amber was a baby, and Harry and I were young, and bacon and eggs were simply what you ate in the morning—every morning. He'd left me a half-pot of decaf, and I was pouring myself a cup when I heard surreptitious noises coming from the den. The door was closed; I eased it open. The sight that greeted me was surreal, like a Cubist painting of a room I'd thought I'd known. Amber had pushed the broken recliner into one corner, and now she was pulling all of Harry's cookbooks and magazines off the shelves. I watched her the way you watch a spectacular bird that flits into your garden, mindless of the fact that it's pulling up all your tomato plants. Blond hair braided in shaggy pigtails. Jeans carefully ripped at each knee. A man's white T-shirt. Bright rings on all her fingers but one, where the diamond from Malvin was missing.

"Daddy's gone for the day, right?" she said.

I nodded uneasily. "What are you doing?"

For an answer, she hurled another stack of magazines to the floor. A cloud of dust rose; she waved it away. "What a pack rat," she said. "Look." She held up a tattered *Gourmet*. "Nineteen seventy-five. I wasn't even *born* in nineteen seventy-five."

The thought of something existing in our lives before she had was clearly baffling to Amber.

"Does Daddy know you're doing this?" I asked.

"Nope." She scrambled up onto the table, stood on tiptoe to reach the top shelf. "It's a surprise. I'm reorganizing. You'll see."

"Great," I said, trying to sound casual. "But, uh, sweetie? Your father's awfully particular about his cookbooks."

"No he isn't." She held up a mangled specimen as proof. "Watch out!" She flung it in my direction; I stepped back just in time. A mushroom cloud of dust rose from the place where it landed.

"Disgusting, isn't it?"

"What's wrong?" I said, expecting pornography.

"Look closer."

I stared at the cover shot: a mixed berry cobbler with whipped cream.

"What?"

"Mites," Amber said grimly.

"Oh," I said weakly. I didn't see any mites, but then again, I'd been thinking that I probably needed bifocals.

"They'll spread through every book if you're not careful. It's a good thing I noticed them. They only seem to be at the top."

"A good thing," I repeated vaguely. I didn't know what to do. This was Harry's den, and these were Harry's mites, and I just didn't think it was a good idea for Amber to be rearranging them without her father's permission. But there was no stopping Amber once she got an idea in her head, and ideas like these occurred to her often whenever she and Malvin split up. She just wanted to help, I understood that. She just wanted to be useful. She was twenty-four years old and brokenhearted and living in her parents' house. One by one, room by room, we'd all fall victim to her various schemes. I remembered the time—was it two or three breakups ago?—when Harry's bootjack had the misfortune of catching her eye. It was made of iron and shaped like a cricket, and Harry loved it dearly, even though he had no boots to be jacked. For years, it had stood unmolested in the laundry room, propping open a warped door, peacefully accumulating dust. Then, one day, after several weeks without Malvin, Amber cleaned the laundry room.

The bootjack vanished.

"You threw out my bootjack?" Harry said, his lower lip trembling like a child's.

"Of course not, Daddy," Amber said, looking horrified. "I gave it to the Salvation Army."

This time, however, she had a point: The den was furnished in odds and ends, the refuge of mites and disintegrating magazines. Harry and I had both been meaning to shovel it out for years. As I got into the car, I decided that, for once, Amber was truly being helpful. She'd alphabetize the cookbooks, sort the magazines into piles, vacuum the corners, and dust the shelves. In the process, she might throw a few things away, but what were a few musty magazines? I pulled out of the driveway, thinking that, perhaps, the breakup with Malvin wasn't entirely bad. I still hoped, of course, that they'd end up back together, but in the meantime, the gutters needed cleaning. The garage needed a fresh coat of paint. Another few weeks, and Amber would have the Kligler homestead in tip-top shape.

The university hospital was in the heart of the downtown district. I'd worked there many years earlier, briefly, before getting my job at Pittsburgh Family Medical. Back then, the hospital had been decorated in the retro-dungeon style, with pale green walls and yellowing floors; cries of misery seemed to drift from behind closed doors. Now I was delighted to see that, much like the rest of Pittsburgh, the place had been gentrified. I scurried through the cold, rainy parking lot to enter a lobby that was warm and bright. Easter decorations were hanging in the windows, and a jungle of potted plants bloomed along one wall. The receptionist actually smiled as she gave me directions to the workshop. Twelfth floor, third door, elevator over to my right.

I had been expecting a large room, perhaps a lecture-style auditorium. A hundred people clutching Styrofoam cups of coffee. A welcome speech, a slide show, a question-and-answer session, followed by a lunch break. Cold-cut platters and more Styrofoam cups. Then, in the afternoon, the inevitable shift to more personal interactions. Maybe an hour spent in small groups talking about—what? Low-carb recipes? The stress of living with a partner who was bouncing out of bed every morning bright-eyed and bushy-tailed? Harry wasn't around as much as he used to be, true, but wasn't that to be expected? Hadn't I urged him to exercise? Wasn't I glad he was suddenly finding as much satisfaction in his work as I'd always found in mine?

I found the third door and opened it with the force you use when you think you're about to enter a large space. I crashed into the back of an older woman's chair; she shot me a dirty look. Surprise—I was in a small conference room. More flowering plants. A large table, a dozen chairs, most of which were already occupied by people who twisted in their seats to look at me. A curl of smoke rose from a cigarette clutched by one of the skinniest human beings I'd ever seen. He glanced at me nervously, then looked away.

"Am I in the right place?" I asked.

"Do you live with someone who just ate a half-pound of bacon for breakfast?" The woman who spoke seemed surprised when people laughed. She was dressed like a lawyer: pin-striped skirt and jacket, hose and heels, the works. "Well, that's what my husband's been eating," she said, sounding miffed.

"Mine, too," said the older woman whose chair I'd bumped. She, too, was nicely dressed. Her shoes, I noticed, had been dyed to match her pink wool skirt and pink wool jacket. "Me, I never touch the stuff. I grew up on a hog farm, and that's enough to sour anybody."

"My wife has tried some weird diets," said the smoking man, "but this one takes the cake."

I slid into a chair beside him, relieved to see he wore jeans. I'd worn sweatpants, a sweatshirt with Tweety Bird on the pocket, and sneakers. I mean, it was the weekend. Who dresses up on a Saturday?

"I don't think you should be smoking in here," said a woman across the table with long, dark hair. She smiled at the skinny man apologetically. The skinny man dropped his cigarette into his can of Coke, exhaled, then lit another from the open pack in front of him.

"You've got to wonder," the pin-striped woman said, "if they're really using this study for what they say they are. I'm glad Larry's lost all this weight, but for all we know, these doctors could be measuring how fast this diet kills a person."

"My wife's gonna die anyway at the rate she's going," said a redheaded man. He was younger than the rest of us, and he wore a sport coat and tie that had both seen better days. "They say she's metabolically resistant. Everybody else is losing fat by the bucketful, but she's only lost fifteen pounds."

"How big is she?" asked the smoking man.

The redheaded man didn't miss a beat. "You ever seen a manatee?"

The women at the table made disapproving clicking sounds with their tongues, but the young man didn't seem to notice.

"Before we got married, I could put my hands around her waist, like this." He demonstrated with his hands. "Then I give her the rock. Bam! She blows up like Shamu."

Even the clickings fizzled after that. Nobody really knew what to say. The woman with the long, dark hair edged her chair away. Then the door opened and Lucy came into the room, and I forgot about the man and his rock and everybody else.

How did I know it was Lucy? (Aside from the name tag, I mean.) Well, I would have recognized Lucy Martin anywhere. We had gone to high school together in Massachusetts. Lucy had been one of those fresh-faced, athletic-looking girls who had a ready smile for everyone—jock or freak, stoner or geek. She still had the same heart-shaped face and sky-blue eyes she'd had at seventeen, and it was clear to me, even now, why my first love, Arnie Grant, had fallen head over heels in love with her the first time she'd looked in his direction. Not that it mattered now. I remembered her crying in the girls' lavatory, telling me how awful she felt, that she'd never meant any of this to happen. I also remembered thinking, Shouldn't *she* be consoling *me*? And, in fact, I'd needed consoling. I continued loving Arnie even after Lucy had thrown him away in favor of the class president's boyfriend—though by then, of course, Arnie no longer gave me the time of day. It was one of the reasons I'd applied to colleges out of state. I remember studying a map of the United States through my tears, and seeing the name of a city that seemed to sum up, in a single word, everything I was feeling.

Pittsburgh.

Perhaps I should have felt gratitude upon seeing Lucy after so many years. She was, after all, the reason I'd found my way into a career instead of settling down to marry at nineteen, the way Arnie ultimately did. The reason I'd met Harry. The reason I sat here, in the middle of a life I knew enough to be grateful for. But as I scanned her up and down, noting the expensive haircut, the size-six slacks and cashmere sweater, the stylish little round purse that was smaller than my billfold alone, what I felt wasn't gratitude. Nope, it was nothing close to gratitude, I was certain of it. So this was Harry's counselor. This was the person to whom he bared his soul for two hours every Thursday night. The person he ate overpriced steaks with afterward. The person about whom he answered, "Oh, she's okay," whenever I asked for particulars.

"Hello, everybody," Lucy said pleasantly, dropping her brief-case beside the last remaining seat. "I'm Lucy Martin-Tousch. I specialize in the psychology of nutrition, and I'm delighted to be making this journey with you and your partners."

She stopped. Sniffed. Pinned the skinny man's cigarette with a look.

"I need you to put that out now," she said. Her voice was calm.

The skinny man dropped it into his Coke can, then automatically lit another.

"Put that one out, too," Lucy said.

He appeared startled. "Sorry," he said. "I just, I can't . . . I mean, it's hard—"

"I understand," Lucy said. She seemed genuinely sympathetic.

The skinny man drowned his freshly lit cigarette, then pushed the rest of the pack toward Lucy. "Here," he said. "You better take these."

I saw that his hands were shaking.

"Thank you," Lucy said. "That must have been difficult for you."

"My wife says you've been teaching them to hypnotize themselves. To help with the cravings?"

This was news to me. Harry had said nothing whatsoever about hypnosis. I narrowed my eyes as Lucy nodded, calmly, as if people hypnotized one another every day.

"Maybe you could hypnotize me, for the smoking. So I could get through this meeting."

Lucy nodded again. Then she did a very peculiar thing. She leaned across the table and told the man a story about a man she knew, a man who wanted to stop smoking. He wanted to stop smoking so very much. He wanted to stop smoking, but what he really, really wanted to do, even more, was rest. He wanted to rest and relax and leave the cigarettes behind. And so she'd suggested that whenever he felt the urge to smoke, he just tap his finger on his knee instead. Wasn't that a good idea? Would he be able to try it? The skinny man nodded and thanked her. He began to tap his knee.

A ripple of comprehension went around our little circle. I wondered how long Lucy had been hypnotizing people. Perhaps she had discovered her talents back in high school. Good God— could she have honed her skills on Arnie?

"At the end of this workshop," she said to the skinny man, though she was speaking to everyone now, "I am going to teach you all a relaxation technique that I hope you'll find useful; whether you're trying to stop smoking, or concentrate better, or simply find a moment of clarity in the midst of a stressful situation. I hope you'll consider it a resource you can draw on whenever you choose. Any major life change puts a strain on

relationships, and a life change involving something as fundamental as eating can really shake up a household. As I'm sure
some of you are noticing."

She smiled, but nobody smiled back.

Good, I thought. Nobody likes you. You're not in high
school anymore.

"An overweight person often believes that if only he or she
were thin, everything else would fall into place. Sometimes partners feel the same way. We think, If he or she weren't so heavy,
we'd go out more. We'd do things together. Our sex life would
be better."

"You can say that again," muttered the redheaded man
who'd been complaining about his wife.

The pin-striped woman made a disgusted sound. The man
shot her a look like, *What did I say?*

"The thing is that once the weight starts coming off, other
problems can surface. I say 'problems,' but I want you to recog-
nize that a problem is not necessarily a negative thing. Sometimes it can be an opportunity."

I stared at my hands. I was going to hate every minute of
this. As soon as Lucy called a break, I was going to make a
run for it. The good news was that she didn't seem to have
recognized me. Thank goodness I'd changed my name when I
married.

"In fact, I'd like to invite you to look at this dietary study as
an opportunity," she was saying, "to grow along with your
partner."

"Grow?" said the redheaded man. "I thought they were
coming here to shrink."

There were a few guffaws, stifled by a few horrified looks.

But now Lucy laughed delightedly. "My goodness, yes," she said, beaming at the man as if he'd just given her a compliment. "Let's hope we'll be able to accomplish that, too."

For the first time, I felt the group's sympathy begin to shift in Lucy's direction. No! I wanted to shout. She's dangerous! Remember, she can hypnotize!

"I speak from experience," Lucy said, "when I tell you that I know what your partners are going through. By the time I was thirty, I weighed two hundred and twenty pounds. My entire life revolved around food—what I was eating, what I wasn't eating, what I was trying not to eat. It almost destroyed my marriage."

Now, like it or not, she held all of us in the palm of her hand.

"Fortunately, I discovered the relationship between carbohydrates and insulin. I also got counseling to help me sort out my emotional relationship with food. In the end, I wound up going back to school and becoming a counselor myself. My life changed for the better, and so, incidentally, did my husband's. I believe your lives will change for the better as well."

This time, her smile was met with smiles.

"Good," she said, and she opened her briefcase and began to pass around a series of photocopies. I recognized the diagram of the pancreas. "I want to make sure you all understand the principles behind low-carb dieting. I'll begin by demonstrating the impact of carbohydrate intake on insulin production."

I had to admit that Lucy was an excellent speaker. I felt as if I were back in PT school, listening to a physiology lecture. We learned how many people with chronic weight problems were, in fact, suffering from insulin intolerance. They had lost the capacity to respond to normal levels of insulin, which meant that the pancreas had to overcompensate, producing more and more in order to regulate blood sugar. Huge amounts of insulin—warning the body to convert sugar to fat—flooded the bloodstream whenever our partners ate oatmeal, rice, corn, bagels, crackers, sweets. Within an hour, their blood sugar would plummet—a direct result of all that insulin. Hungry again, they reached for a muffin, a banana, a caffeinated soda. It was this vicious cycle that had led them into obesity.

"How many of you have partners who began this diet with high triglycerides?" Lucy asked.

Almost everyone raised a hand.

"How many high cholesterol?"

More hands.

"Abnormal glucose tests?"

Everybody had a hand in the air.

"And what are their levels now?"

We went around the room. It was funny—I knew Harry's latest blood chemistries the way I knew his Social Security number. In three months, his triglycerides had dropped from 3200 to 450. His *total* cholesterol was down to 245—still high, but nowhere near what it had been. His fasting blood sugar was on the high end of normal. Even the redheaded man whose wife was metabolically resistant acknowledged that her bad cholesterol and triglycerides had dropped, and that—oddly enough—her gout had cleared up.

Almost before I knew it, the cold-cut platters had appeared.

"Lunch!" Lucy announced brightly. She smiled at me as I scuttled off to the ladies' room, the sort of pleasant smile you give a stranger. I decided not to mention anything to Harry about having known her before. What did it matter now? Water under the bridge. Lucy was competent, interesting, encouraging. She had also been through this herself, which gave her a lot of credibility—even when she used the sort of feel-good jargon that made me cringe. I supposed that if Harry lost sixty or seventy pounds by July, I'd be so grateful that it wouldn't even matter that his nutritional counselor had broken my teenage heart.

My opinion of Lucy rose again that afternoon, when the focus shifted—just as I'd expected—to our own anxieties, expectations, and fears. As it turned out, I didn't even have to say anything. The other people in the group were dying to talk. Fine by me. I watched the woman in the pink wool suit weep silently as she spoke of her husband's blood pressure, his refusal to take his health seriously, her fear of losing him forever. The smoking man talked about his wife's decision to give up smoking after doctors found a lump in her breast, how she made it through radiation and chemo, how happy she was when food began to taste good to her again. Only now she was eating the way that she'd once smoked, the way he still smoked—constantly, compulsively.

"You'd think I could give it up," he said, tapping away madly with his finger, "but I can't."

The last person to speak was the redheaded man we'd all come to despise. He talked about how he felt his entire life was going to hell. How he'd been laid off from two successive jobs and how he now worked twice as hard for less pay. How he'd wanted a family, but his wife had had three miscarriages, and now she didn't want to risk getting pregnant again. How his parents had died within six months of each other. How the car needed a new transmission. How he hadn't shoveled the sidewalk in months, and the city had sent him a citation, and—

Lucy suggested that his wife's weight might be a kind of symbol for all the other things in his life he couldn't control.

The man began to sob. "I want to help her," he said, "but

I'm just making everything worse, watching every damn thing she puts in her mouth."

For the first time all day, people were looking at him as if he were something other than a reptile. The long-haired woman even put a hand on his arm. Lucy talked about the importance of recognizing the way our minds make symbols out of things, how we shouldn't allow our partner's weight to become something larger than it already was.

"No pun intended," the redheaded man said, wiping his eyes.

Everybody laughed.

We concluded with a relaxation exercise in which we simply closed our eyes and concentrated on our breathing. How it came in cool through our noses and exited warm through our mouths. How it carried away any tension we were feeling. How it grounded us in the here and now.

"This has been a great workshop," Lucy said as we packed up our things to go. As I passed her chair, she smiled at me encouragingly. "I hope this was helpful for you," she said. "Francie, isn't it?"

I froze, but there was nothing in her face except the same generic goodwill she'd been showing everyone. "Francie," I agreed, speaking in a voice that was nothing like my own.

Lucy dug around in her little round purse and pulled out a silver case. "Here," she said, handing me a business card. "You were the only person who didn't speak today. If you think of something, feel free to give me a call."

"Thanks," I squeaked, taking the card and dumping it into the void at the bottom of my purse. Outside in the parking lot, I breathed a little sigh of relief. Lucy hadn't recognized me. I was safe.

9

I had a few errands to run on my way home from the hospital. I picked up the dry-cleaning. I stopped at the butcher. I
dashed into the co-op for some greens. Yes, Pittsburgh has a co-
op. We have a lovely farmer's market, as well. Believe me, we've
come a long way since the era of steel mills and slaughter-
houses. The Cathedral of Knowledge still looms over the city
like a haunted house, but we have plenty of architecture that
doesn't frighten children. We have lovely riverside parks and
terrific restaurants. We have top-rate universities and a wonderful science museum. We have charming little neighborhoods
lined with sweet brick bungalows, and tonight, for the sheer
pleasure of it, I avoided the interstate, winding my way through
the side streets until I reached our house.

Lulled by the warm afterglow of the workshop, thinking
about my breath coming in cool and exiting warm, I didn't
immediately notice the two pickup trucks parked along the
curb. Each had an extendable ladder strapped to its side, and
the beds were filled with a clutter of tools, two-by-fours, pieces
of Sheetrock. On the side of one was a logo: INSTA-GYM:
REMODELING DONE IN A DAY. It was then that the house itself
caught my eye. It looked different, though in a way that was
hard to explain. Something about the droop of the curtains in
the front windows. Something about the way the light behind
them seemed too bright. An enormous garbage pile spilled into

the street—had it been there when I left in the morning? Drawing closer, I suddenly realized it wasn't garbage at all. It was the contents of Harry's den: the recliner, the exercise bike, the long table he'd used as his desk. I felt my heart sink: There were cookbooks and magazines, too. Rolls of indoor-outdoor carpet. Pretty much everything that had been in the room, except his computer—though who could say? Amber was nothing if not thorough. Perhaps the computer was at the bottom of the pile.

For the first time, I noticed Harry's car, idling at a crazy angle in the driveway, the driver's-side door slightly open. The front door leading into the house was open, too. I parked and got out. Shrill voices drifted into the darkness like sparks from a raging fire. I took the precaution of turning off Harry's car and pocketing the keys before heading up the steps. The kitchen was empty, and so was the living room. The drama seemed to be unfolding in the den. I opened the door and found not only Harry and Amber, but Malva Miracle, Krys Placek, and four hulking men wearing tool belts and paint-splattered jeans.

Everybody seemed to be talking at once. In the midst of them all stood Jason, who was attempting to referee. The room that had been here when I'd left this morning had vanished like Brigadoon. In its place was, well, another country, a land of white walls and track lighting and freshly laid carpeting. A stainless-steel desk with a Herman Miller chair sat beside a wall of stainless-steel shelves. These shelves held roughly half the cookbooks that had been there before, making room for a TV, a VCR, and a selection of exercise videos. Looking around, I glimpsed a spanking new exercise bike, a StairMaster, and a miniature trampoline. There were free weights. There was a boom box with detachable speakers. Actually, there were two of each of these things, thanks to the mirrors that now covered one wall.

Amber had transformed the den into a home gym, a state-of-the-art exercise studio. At least she had kept the computer. It was sitting, unmolested, in the middle of the new desk.

"What I hear you saying, Amber," Jason said in a voice that seemed older than his own, "is that you don't feel Dad appreciates all the trouble you took to surprise him."

"You never used this room anymore," Amber cried. Her pale skin had gone blotchy with despair. "You're never even home! I thought it would be nice if you could exercise here instead of always going to the gym!"

"My desk! Fifteen years' worth of books!"

"It wasn't a desk, it was a wobbly old table! And your books are right here. I only got rid of the ones that were falling apart. I even tried to donate them to the library, but they said they were worthless because—"

"They were *not* worthless to me!"

"What I hear you saying, Dad, is that you wish Amber had respected—" Jason began, but Malva cut him off.

"Listen, Harold. Done is done. Lighten up before you rupture something vital."

"Lighten up?" Krys said. My goodness, she *had* lost weight "How would you like it if Malvin moved home and rearranged your life to suit himself?"

"I didn't do it for myself," Amber wailed, but Malva ignored her, planting herself in front of Krys.

"*If* Malvin moved home?" Malva said. Now her voice rose, too. "*If?* Where the hell do you think my son has been for the last two weeks?"

This was news to me. I could tell it was news to Amber as well.

"Every night, I walk in the door and there he stands, complaining about my furniture. Go on home, I tell him, but he says he's lonely, he's confused, he's going to hang with me until he figures out the next step. Maybe, says he, I can help you with some renovations. Baby, says I, no offense, but I don't care to live in a place that looks like the inside of a microwave. So what does he do? Pulls up my nice green Formica counter and puts in a slab of some butt-ugly rock. *Expensive* butt-ugly rock."

Malva spun back to Amber, who was smiling in spite of herself, her gaze gone soft with affection.

"You children need to make nice before you tear this whole neighborhood to pieces! Your daddy's cookbooks, my nice Formica. Don't you think this has gone far enough?"

An enormous tear made its way down Amber's cheek. In the silence that followed, the largest of the hulking men spoke. "So who plans to pay for this work that nobody seems to want?"

"I do," Harry and Amber said in unison.

The hulking man snorted. "*Both* of you can pay me, then. Now, for the love of Pete, would you all get the hell out of here? We need to finish up."

"Anyone for coffee?" I said from the door.

Everybody spun around to look at me. The carpenters exchanged glances. "Who's she?" one of them hissed.

"Does it matter?"

"Christ, we're gonna be here all night."

"Coffee," I repeated. "In the kitchen. I'm making a pot right now."

I led the way and, after a moment, everyone followed. Malva kept her arm around Amber, while Krys tended to Harry, who staggered slightly like a man in shock. Jason came last, looking absolutely drained. "Nothing you read about conflict resolution can prepare you for something like this," he muttered, then stomped upstairs to his room. We all heard his bedroom door slam, even above the noise the carpenters were making as they put the final touches on the den, or the gym, or whatever it was called now. Somehow the sound of that slamming door had a sobering effect on everybody. Jason had never slammed a door in his life. Remorse settled on everyone like a fine mist as I turned on the coffeepot.

"I just wanted to do something nice for you, Daddy," Amber said, sniffling. "You said you wanted to develop other talents. I didn't know those books meant that much to you anymore."

"I know," Harry said. "It was just . . . a shock."

Malva snorted. "Once this girl gets an idea, she doesn't execute halfway. Ask Malvin if you don't believe me."

"I believe you," Harry said.

Amber blushed miserably. "There are two sides to every story," she said, to no one in particular.

In the next room, the carpenters let loose with a flurry of hammering.

"There are two *hundred* sides to every story," Malva replied. "But all of them end the same. Somebody has to apologize."

Mercifully, the hammering ceased. The coffeemaker wheezed and sighed. I brought Harry an early cup and nudged it, steaming, into his hands. The look on his face made me feel like a Red Cross relief worker. And, like a relief worker, I realized there was only so much I could do.

"Maybe we can salvage some of the books," I suggested, but a glance out the window told me I was wrong. It had started to rain, a cold, steady spring rain, the kind of rain that beats away the last gray traces of snow along the highways. A rain that seeps deep into the earth to touch sleeping bulbs and dormant roots. A rain that would pound what remained of

Harry's tattered books into pulp. I sat down, suddenly feeling very tired.

Harry understood. "At least she didn't throw *all* of them away."

"There's the spirit," Malva said.

"Tell me what happened," I said. "From the beginning."

Harry looked at Amber; Amber looked at Krys; Krys looked at Malva.

Malva went first.

"I went out to get the mail, oh, about four-thirty," Malva said, "and I happen to look down the street and what do I see? Harry's car all crooked in the driveway, the door hanging open, no one in sight. Lord, I thought, that crazy new diet has given him a heart attack. But no, he's in here yelling, and Amber's yelling, and Jason and Krys are standing there like they don't know what to do."

"I'd thought the house was being robbed," Krys said. "Or someone was carjacked or something."

"It sounded like a carjacking," Malva agreed.

I was glad that I'd missed the bulk of it, and I admitted as much as I got up to pour coffee for the rest of us.

"I must say, it's an awfully nice little gym," Malva said as we all settled down around the kitchen table.

"I'd use it every day if it were mine," Krys said.

"You look as if that's what you've been doing," I told her. "Really, Krys, you look great."

She beamed at me, and I realized with a start how very pretty she was. "You've lost some weight, too, haven't you?"

I nodded. "Side effect of Harry's diet."

"He's a good influence."

"Isn't he!" Malva said, looking him up and down. "I've got to hand it to you, Harry. You're only half the man you used to be."

"Three-quarters, anyway," Harry said, but he still wasn't ready to smile. Instead, he turned to Amber. "Dumpling," he said. "Listen. I'm sorry I got so upset."

She was playing with her coffee cup. "You *do* like it a little bit, don't you?"

"It was very generous," Harry said, avoiding the question. "Too generous. You shouldn't be spending your money on me. You should put it toward buying a house of your own or . . ."

He glanced at Malva, then stopped, considered his options.

"Or whatever you decide to do next," he finished.

"She's already decided," Malva informed us.

"Have I?" Amber stuck out her chin.

"First, she's gonna hunt around for the biggest olive branch she can find. Then she's gonna drag it over to my house and knock on the door."

Amber shook her head. "What's the point? He wouldn't accept it if I did."

"Be reasonable," I urged her. "It was a long trip home from Jamaica."

A gleam appeared in Amber's eyes. "Good."

"Dumpling," Harry said.

"Sorry."

"Now, see?" Malva said. "That wasn't so hard. You keep on practicing."

A knock at the door interrupted Amber's reply, and Mr. Polk stepped into the kitchen. "Is this a private party?" he asked.

"Clearly not," I said. "Want coffee?"

He sniffed the air hopefully. "The hazelnut kind?"

"Could be."

"If it ain't too much trouble." He sat down at the table, unzipped his coat. "So what's all the commotion? Something catch fire?"

"Not exactly," I said.

"Then what's all that trash out front?"

Harry winced.

"I cleaned out Dad's den," Amber explained.

Mr. Polk squinted at Harry as if he were seeing him for the first time. "Hoo, boy!" he said. "Losin' some of that baby fat, ain't ya? Whatchoo been livin' on, celery and sawdust?"

Harry managed a weak smile.

"His celery and sawdust are restricted," I said. "This is a different kind of diet."

"A diet is a diet," Malva sniffed. "Diet food is diet food."

"This diet food is delicious," Krys said.

"That so?" Mr. Polk eyed Krys with a look of flat-out disbelief. "Well, let me be the judge of that." He turned to Harry. "Invite me to stay to dinner."

"Sounds like you just invited yourself," I said.

"Whatever's gonna get me a taste of Harry's cooking," Mr. Polk said. "How long has it been? Hell, I've missed y'all."

"I've missed you, too," Malva said. "When was the last time we all sat around this table?"

"New Year's Day," Krys said. "Can you believe it?"

Everybody looked at Harry.

"Actually," I said, coming to his rescue, "Harry's been taking a little vacation from the kitchen."

Mr. Polk looked stricken. "For how long?"

"Until I get my weight to where it ought to be," Harry explained. "It's easier if I'm not always being tempted."

"Then who's been cooking? Not Francie!" Malva said.

"Hey," I said, insulted.

"She's doing great," Harry said.

"Fact is," Mr. Polk said, "I don't care which-a-one of you cooks tonight. I don't even care if you serve up a big nasty bowl of lettuce. It's the company that matters."

"True, true," Malva agreed.

"What do you say? Should I holler up Mari and Beth?"

Harry and I looked at each other.

"Do we have enough food for nine people?" Harry asked.

I opened the freezer. We had six steaks, a pack of chicken breasts, two pounds of frozen hot dogs, and a cube of frozen spinach. We had gin and sugar-free tonic water. We had the organic greens I'd picked up at the co-op.

"Sure," I said.

Krys ran home to settle the girls while Mr. Polk collected Mari and Beth, who—it turned out—had also noticed Harry's car and were about to come over, anyway. I whipped up a pitcher of martinis to dull the pain as we waited for the steaks to broil, the chicken to fry, the hot dogs to boil, and the spinach to steam. Together, we told and retold the story of The Gym, honing it until it was smooth and sharp, until even Harry and Amber were laughing. And by the time we sat down to eat, Jason had been coaxed from his room.

"Pass the salt?" he asked Malva, who replied, "I hear you saying, Jason, that your beef isn't seasoned exactly to your taste."

Everybody howled, but Jason took it well. Malva stood up and proposed a toast to the future Dr. Kligler. Amber leaned across the table to kiss her brother on the cheek. "You were great, 'Tart," she told him. "A real professional."

Jason beamed.

*   *   *

BY HALF PAST eight, everyone had left, even the carpenters. Amber grabbed the bill before Harry or I could see it and headed upstairs to her room. But she surprised us by reappearing ten minutes later in a pink cashmere sweater and black jeans. Her hair was smoothed into a loose twist. Her lips were bright with lipstick.

"I'm going out for a while," was all she said.

Harry, Jason, and I rushed to the front window. Sure enough, she hadn't taken the Mercedes. She was walking up the street toward Malva's house under a sleek black umbrella.

"Thank God," I said.

"Not so fast," Harry said. "I give them ten minutes and she's back."

"Five bucks says twenty," Jason said.

"Hey, guys," I protested, but they ignored me and shook on it anyway before Jason excused himself to go call Mary Elizabeth. The rain was falling even harder now, shining on the street like ice. The pile of things on the lawn appeared to have deflated. Monday morning, the city would haul everything off to the dump.

"Well," Harry said, resigned. "Want to check out the new den?"

The den was actually nicely done, once you got used to it. We stared at ourselves in the mirrored wall. We made faces. I pulled a few exercise videos off the shelves and together we studied their jackets. Suzanne Somers was Somersizing. Jane Fonda was doing something with her legs that seemed physically impossible.

"Would you look at that," Harry said.

"Stop drooling. Dibs on the trampoline."

"Dibs on the StairMaster."

"Really? Those things are murder."

"Piece of cake," Harry said, climbing aboard.

I kicked off my shoes and got on the trampoline. "Dinner was fun, wasn't it?" I said, bouncing.

Harry punched a button and for a moment the StairMaster slowed. "This thing really gets you in the thighs," he said.

"Just like old times," I said, doing a half turn in between jumps. "Everybody in the kitchen."

Harry punched another button.

"Did you have any idea that Malvin had moved back home?"

"Nope."

I attempted a full turn. Missed. "I wonder if he and Amber are working things out as we speak."

Harry kept on stepping. He hadn't asked me one question about my time with Lucy.

It occurred to me that I'd been working awfully hard at this conversation with very little return on my investment. And this was not an isolated incident. More and more, it seemed to me that Harry wasn't really listening when I spoke. Our bodies might be located in the same room, but his mind was someplace far away. I bounced some more. Fine. I'd just wait for him to say something to me. But I am not, by nature, the silent type, and this was more easily said than done. For a while, there was only the sound of the StairMaster, the squeak of the trampoline. I bounced higher. I endured. Then I began to have doubts. Maybe he was legitimately upset with me. Maybe I had done something wrong.

"Is something the matter, Harry?"

"What?" He seemed surprised. "No."

I waited for him to ask why I'd asked. He didn't.

"Then why are you so quiet?"

"I have a lot on my mind, that's all."

"So tell me what's on your mind," I said. "And don't say 'the IPO.'"

"The IPO."

Harry grinned, but I was not amused.

"Harry!"

"Well, it's true."

"Do you think it's healthy? Thinking about work all the time?"

Harry stepped harder. I tried again.

"Wouldn't you feel, well, kind of lonely if all I ever thought about was rehabilitating joints?"

Harry kept on stepping.

"Because lately all we seem to talk about is your job."

"So I'm boring you," Harry said, without expression.

"You know I don't mean that," I said. "I just wish that sometimes we could talk about other things."

"Fine." Beads of sweat had broken out across his forehead. "What do you want to talk about?"

I stopped myself mid-bounce and stepped off the trampoline. What on earth was I doing? Our first evening to ourselves in weeks, and here I was, picking a fight! And yet I was only being honest. I was only saying things that needed to be said. I took a moment to focus on my breath coming in cool through my nose and exiting warm through my mouth, the way Lucy had suggested. Then I forged ahead.

"I just wish we could talk the way we used to, you know?

Lately you've been putting so much energy into your job, and . . . well, I'm proud of your accomplishments, you know that. But I was here for you, your family was here, long before you started talking about IPOs and yachts."

Harry hopped off the StairMaster. "For Pete's sake, Francie," he said, "I was joking about the yachts."

All my deep breaths—in as well as out—were starting to feel hot. "Stop misunderstanding me on purpose!"

"Look." Harry mopped his face with his shirtsleeve. "You wanted me to lose weight, so I'm losing weight. You wanted me to stop cooking and develop other interests, so I did."

"*I* wanted? What happened to what *we* wanted? We both agreed that you needed to change your lifestyle!"

"And that's what I'm doing. Only now you're mad because I'm getting involved at work instead of spending all my time hanging around the kitchen."

"You're not involved. You're obsessed. You're hardly ever home anymore, and when you are, you're far away."

"I'm standing right here in front of you, Francie."

He sounded every bit as frustrated as I felt, and this mollified me a little. At least he was reacting. If he was reacting, that meant he was listening.

"I just worry that you're changing," I said.

"And I worry"—Harry's voice was barely audible—"that you're not."

I stared at him, stung. "You want *me* to change?" I said. "Since when?"

"Francie," Harry said. Then he sighed. "Sweetheart. What I want is for you to stop making a big deal out of nothing. I don't want to fight with you, okay?"

He sounded like he meant it.

"I don't want to fight with you, either," I said, miserably. I stepped toward him, but instead of hugging me, he moved aside, patting my shoulder.

"I'm a sweaty mess," he said. "I'm going to take a shower."

"You won't even hug me!"

"Francie, come on!" He was really mad now. "This is what I mean about making something out of nothing."

"Am I?" I said. "Do you know how long it's been since we've made love?"

As soon as I'd said it, I realized that this was what I'd been wanting to say all along. Harry looked away from me, but I caught his eye in the mirror. We glared at each other in the long, mirrored wall.

"I'm sorry if fighting doesn't put me in the mood," he said with unbearable calm. "I'm going to take my shower now."

He turned away.

I should have gone after him. I should have waited until I heard the water running, then slipped off my clothes and followed him into the steam. I should have let our bodies forgive each other, no need for words or apologies. But that night, for some reason, I couldn't. We couldn't. In the morning, of course, we both apologized.

But by then it was too late.

PART THREE

The Perfect Storm

I O

"So how is Harry?" Tommy asked, smearing a generous lump of cream cheese onto his bagel.

It was late in the afternoon, and we'd run across the street to the Bagel Baron, grabbing a seat by a window that overlooked the lurch and stop of passing traffic. It felt good to get out of the clinic and into the bright May sunshine. I had a patient in fifteen minutes, but I'd lost my lunch hour to a last-minute appointment involving bilateral knee injuries. The patient, a man in his thirties, had been riding in a taxicab. "Where's the seat belt?" he'd asked the driver, who'd replied, "Not to worry, pal, you got no need for that when you're with me."

That was the last thing my patient remembered.

"Harry is Harry," I said noncommittally. "He's into this major project at work. I barely see him these days."

My bagel was huge and soft, glistening with garlic crumbs, throbbing with carbohydrates. Guiltily, I glanced out the window and fought the urge to duck down in my seat, just in case Harry happened to drive by. But even if he did, so what? I could certainly have a bagel once in a while if I wanted to.

I took an enormous bite.

"It must be nice to have Amber out of the house," Tommy said.

"Actually, I kind of miss her," I said. I hadn't seen much of her since she moved back into Malvin's condo. "Not that I want her living with us again anytime soon."

"At least you've got Jason."

I chewed hard. "Between Mary Elizabeth and college plans, he's already got one foot out the door."

Jason had been chosen to attend an accelerated premed summer program, which meant he'd be leaving for Stanford only a few days after graduation. Lately, he'd taken to wearing his Stanford baseball cap everywhere he went. He slept in his Stanford T-shirt. Sentences that did not begin with "Mary Elizabeth says . . ." began with "At Stanford, they . . ."

In a way, he was already gone.

"I can't imagine Sue-Sue leaving for college," Tommy said. "It's bad enough having her across town. Jessica tells me she's already got her eye on NYU. Won't even *consider* Penn State." He sighed.

"How is Jessica?" I asked.

"Very, very happy." Tommy wiped his mouth on a napkin.

"Why?"

"I suspect it has to do with seeing less of me."

I didn't know what to say.

"I'm sorry," Tommy said. "That came out bitter. I don't want things to be that way. It's just, well . . ." Abruptly, he glanced at his watch. "Do you need to get back?"

"I'm okay," I said. "They'll beep me."

"It's just that she bought this couch," he said. "It's big, it's white, it's fluffy. It's got about a hundred little pillows. I saw it last weekend when I dropped Sue-Sue off."

"And?"

"Well, it's bugging me. I mean, if somebody had said, 'Here are a hundred couches. For one million dollars, pick the couch your wife would be *least* likely to pick,' well, that's the one I'd have chosen."

"People change," I said awkwardly.

"I didn't change," Tommy said firmly. Then: "What about you? Would you say you've changed? I mean, since you got married?"

I thought about the fight I'd had with Harry.

"Not fundamentally, no," I admitted. "I'm the same as I've always been."

We sat together in silence. A little cloud descended over each of us, blocking out the bright sunshine, the clamor of conversations, the rattle of paper bags. I knew exactly what he'd meant about the couch. It was the way I'd felt about Harry's new underwear. I'd been folding laundry when I discovered half a dozen pairs of brand-new Jockeys. I hadn't looked at them closely; I'd just assumed they were Jason's. I left them in a colorful heap on Jason's bed. But Jason brought them back to me, saying, "These aren't mine, they must be Dad's."

"Oh," I'd said lightly, but I'd been stunned. Even in college, Harry had been a dedicated boxer man. His tastes ran toward solid, conservative colors, whites and pale blues and grays. These new Jockeys were red and green and yellow. Two pairs were striped. One was paisley. If someone had promised me a million dollars to choose the pair *Harry* would be least likely to wear, I would have chosen the paisley. I would have bet my life on it.

What if Harry and I were becoming like Tommy and Jessica? What if Harry changed so much he left me far behind?

"Can I ask you something?" I said to Tommy. "It's kind of a medical question."

"Shoot."

"Can a change in diet affect someone's personality?"

"You're talking about Harry?"

I nodded.

Tommy considered the question seriously. "Change in what way?"

"It's hard to explain," I said. "It's—"

To my horror, I realized I was about to cry.

"Sorry," I said, crumbling up my napkin and pressing it to my eyes. "I'm glad he's losing weight and everything, but—" I blew my nose, trying to act as if crying in front of a colleague in a public place was no big deal. "When he comes home from work, he detaches. It's like a light clicking off. There's this incredible . . . *distance.*"

"I suppose it could be a thyroid condition," Tommy said. "Prolonged dieting of any kind can have that effect. Any changes in his skin or hair?"

I shook my head. "Nothing like that. It's just that he's so busy all the time. He's working sixty hours a week. He goes out with people in his support group. He goes for walks before work. I just wish he could find the energy—"

My beeper chose that moment to buzz.

"Let it wait," Tommy said. I wished he would stop looking at me. There are people who cry gracefully. I am not one of those people.

"No, it's okay. I'm okay," I said.

"Do you really think it's the diet?"

"I guess not," I admitted.

"Neither do I. You know why?"

I shook my head.

"Because that's how Jessica was. Leave for work: click on. Come home: click off. And I was like you. I kept making excuses. I kept telling myself it was because she'd given up drinking coffee."

My beeper buzzed again. "I have to go," I said.

"Don't just hope this will go away," Tommy said. "That's what I did, and now it's too late for Jess and me."

"Are you sure?" I asked.

"Probably," he said. Then he sighed. "Maybe not."

"I hope not," I said, and I meant it with all my heart. "I hope . . ." But I could feel the tears coming again. I stood up and Tommy stood up, too. Our thighs bumped the table. Poppy seeds scattered everywhere.

"Francie?" Tommy said.

"I've got to go," I said, digging through my purse. "Here, let me get this."

"I already got it."

"You got it the last time." I dredged a ten-dollar bill out of the depths of a zippered pocket and pushed it into his hand as a business card tumbled to the floor. Lucy's card. I'd forgotten all about it. I picked it up and shoved it back into my pocket.

"Thanks for listening," I said.

"C'mon," he said. "You listen to me enough." To my surprise, he leaned over the table and hugged me, a quick, awkward hug. His cheek against mine was surprisingly smooth. "Talk to him," he said again. "I'm speaking from experience. If the lamp clicks off, remember: You can always yank the chain."

✻　　✻　　✻

I DID TRY to talk to Harry. I tried to yank that chain. I tried as the days grew longer and the sun grew stronger. I tried as the daffodils were replaced by tulips, as the tulips yielded to irises and the hard, pink buds of peonies. I tried as the robins reappeared, as the grass turned green and greener still. I tried to talk to him in the morning, as he dressed in the new thirty-six-waist pants I'd gotten him for his forty-eighth birthday. I tried in the evening, after he came home from Group, or from yet another late night at the office.

"You go ahead," he'd say when I'd ask if he was ready for bed. "I'm not tired."

Or: "I just want to finish reading this."

Or: "I've been around people all day, Francie. I just need some downtime, that's all."

How do you address a problem with someone who insists there *isn't* a problem? Yes, he agreed, he *was* busy, he *was* distracted, but that was just because of the IPO. Didn't I understand that he was doing this for us? If the IPO went through, our privately held employee stock would be traded on the Nasdaq in the fall. If everything held together. If everybody came through. There were still VCs to lock down. There were still some legal issues with the patent office. There was still a final client to get on board. And, of course, there was the matter of the market itself.

"It's a long shot," Harry said. "But if this happens, our lives could really change."

He didn't seem to realize that our lives had already changed.

Several times, I took Lucy's business card out of my coat pocket. *Call me if you ever want to talk.* But what if my voice jogged her memory? What if she figured out who I was? Besides, it wasn't as if Harry and I were mad at each other, exactly. It wasn't as if one of us had done something wrong. It was just that we didn't have time to talk and laugh together. We didn't have time to relax. And then there was that other thing we didn't have time for, either. It loomed between us during the day, stretched out in bed between us at night.

I had, as Malva would have put it, embarked on a trip down *de Nile*. Despite all evidence to the contrary, I told myself that everything would be fine. Another few weeks and Jason would graduate. Harry would complete the dietary study. He'd have his board meeting, and the IPO would go ahead—or it wouldn't. Either way, we'd have our lives back again. So what if we hadn't gotten around to planning anything elaborate for our anniversary? Maybe the thing to do was simply rent a car and head for the Poconos. We'd hike and swim and sleep late into the morning, and by the time we came back, we'd have found our way back to each other. We'd have fallen in love all over again. What better time than now? Harry had shed ten years along with the extra weight. People looked at him differently. Women looked at him differently. Women *looked* at him—I couldn't help but notice. It hadn't happened for a while. When you're married to somebody who is one hundred pounds overweight, inner beauty isn't the first thing that the other women notice.

It was my mother who finally suggested to me that Harry was having an affair.

I I

*M*y mother came, as promised, to Jason's graduation party. The twins came, too. So did Amber and Malvin, of course, and Malva and the rest of the neighborhood, and Harry's parents, and at least a dozen friends and teachers from school. We rented a tent, set it up in the backyard. There were flowers and balloons. There was a fortune-teller. There were white linens and glass champagne flutes spread across three long tables. Amber and Malvin paid for it all. They would have paid for catering, too, if Jason had not made it clear that he wanted Harry and me to cook his graduation meal. *Together.* It seemed to me that he placed special emphasis on that final word.

"We'd love to," I said, delighted at the thought of Harry back in the kitchen. Certainly, it was time. I'd broached the subject myself, but Harry had insisted that he wasn't ready yet. He was still losing weight. He wanted to finish the diet study first. He wanted to get the IPO behind him. I had to admit he barely had enough time to *eat* a meal these days, much less cook one. But when Jason asked, Harry didn't hesitate.

"Anything you want, 'Tart. Low-carb food or regular?"

"Low-carb," Jason said. "Except the cake."

"A sheet cake or something more elaborate?"

"I don't care as long as there's frosting."

"You got it. What about the main course?"

"Shish kebabs?" Jason suggested.

"Excellent, sir," Harry said. "May we recommend lamb? In a lime marinade?"

"Can you make some of them vegetarian? Mary Elizabeth doesn't eat meat."

"You mean we're actually going to meet this girl?"

"Uh," Jason said, and he colored a bit. "She's eighteen."

Harry stared at him blankly.

"She's a woman, not a girl," I explained. Jason had already coached me on the subject. Mary Elizabeth's politics, it appeared, required significant coaching.

Harry colored, too. "Oh," he said. "Sure."

"And Mom?" Jason said quickly. "Maybe you could make a big tossed salad with cherry tomatoes? And your great coleslaw? And that low-carb potato salad thing you make, but without potatoes. You know, it's got mayonnaise in it?"

I looked at him. "Cauliflower salad?"

"That's it."

Harry's eyes met mine. "Our gourmet offspring," he said, and both of us smiled, a true shared smile. Jason might be dating an eighteen-year-old woman, but this was our boy, our baby. There was nothing, in that moment, that we wouldn't have done—for him, or for each other.

The morning of graduation dawned sunny and warm and perfect. Harry surprised me with a corsage, and the gesture was so thoughtful, so absolutely unexpected, that I forgave him— almost—when he told me he needed to run to the office after the graduation ceremony, just for an hour, to deal with a couple of last-minute faxes. He'd be home by three o'clock at the latest. The party didn't start till six. He'd get the shish kebabs done in plenty of time; it would be no problem. The lamb was already marinating. It was just a matter of cutting up the veggies.

"What about the cake?"

"It's just a simple sheet cake," Harry said. "No big deal."

"No big deal?" I'd expected nothing less than a selection of cakes: a caramel cake, perhaps, drowning in burnt-sugar icing; devil's food with butter cream; maybe even a peppermint chiffon. "Harry, it's your son's graduation. It's your first time back in the kitchen in months. I can't believe you're making a cake that's *no big deal*."

"It's a spice cake," Harry said defensively. "With *frosting*. Which is all Jason wanted, remember? Plus it's fast and easy, and it doubles well."

"Since when do you choose a recipe because it's fast and easy?"

"Since this graduation party got scheduled for the same week that we finalize the marketing budget."

"You mean you scheduled your marketing meeting for the same week as Jason's graduation."

"I don't have any control over it, Francie. This is when we could get everybody together. Look, I said I'd make a cake, and I'm making a cake. Why does everything have to be an argument?"

It was a question I'd been trying to answer myself.

At nine in the morning, Amber and Malvin pulled into the driveway with Trish and Tina in the backseat. Even I, their own mother, was struck by how very much alike they looked. Smooth, light-brown hair. Almond-shaped eyes. For a moment, in fact, as they got out of the car, I truly couldn't tell who was who, and I experienced the same awful, sinking feeling I'd felt when they were little girls and I caught one passing for the other. At those times, I could only wonder how often they'd impersonated each other successfully—and to what effect. Had Trish, who didn't like to swallow pills, convinced Tina to take her medicine?

Had Tina, who hated needles, convinced Trish—the brave one—to get inoculated twice?

I'd wanted them to stay with Harry and me, of course, but they'd opted for Malvin and Amber's.

"Nothing personal, Mom," Tina had said, "but Grandma Sylvia's already staying with you guys, and it's—"

"Kind of cramped?" Trisha had finished.

"Plus, you know, Grandma Sylvia's—"

"Kind of intense?"

My mother appeared beside me now, clutching a cup of coffee. Her makeup was perfect. Her hair was sprayed and teased into a shiny blond dome. Unfortunately, she still hadn't dressed, and the silk bathrobe she wore—embroidered with dragons—was cut to show a fair amount of cleavage. It was very nice cleavage, too. Her legs were as smooth and shapely as they'd been when I was a girl.

Together, we stood in the doorway, watching the kids walk up the drive, waiting for the moment when they'd look up and see us. My mother groped for her bifocals, raised them to her nose like a customs official inspecting produce for weevils. Trish and Tina wore matching purple hemp jumpers, brown Birkenstocks like Tommy's. Beside them, Amber shimmered in Versace, one hand draped over Malvin's arm.

"Don't the girls look great?" I said, unable to squelch a burst of pride.

"What?" My mother lowered her glasses to give me a disbelieving stare, then raised them to her eyes again. "I was looking at Malvin. Can't you just imagine those long legs wrapped around your body?"

Oh, God.

"Uh, Mom?" I said. "Maybe you'd better get dressed."

My mother fixed me with a look of warm amusement, and then, dragons rippling, stepped past me onto the porch. "Coming?" she asked. Then: "Hello! How are my girls?"

She hugged Trish and Tina briskly before seizing her darling Amber. Released, the twins fell on me like puppies. As I wrapped my arms around them both, inhaling the scent of patchouli, I could hear my mother telling Malvin, in purring tones, that he looked good enough to eat.

"Down, Grandma," Amber said.

Malvin laughed, unperturbed. He'd recently dyed his hair a butternut shade of blond that emphasized his smooth, dark skin, and he wore a pale green suit that would have looked effeminate on any other man. I supposed he was used to women throwing themselves at him.

"So where's the 'Tart Man?" he asked.

The 'Tart Man, it turned out, was in the kitchen with Harry, stiff-shouldered in his new suit. The twins gaped.

"Pop-Tart's so big," Tina cried, "and Daddy, you're—"

"So thin," Trish finished.

"You look fantastic!" they exclaimed in unison.

"I told you I had lost weight," Harry said as he and Jason struggled to keep their balance beneath the twins' exuberant hugs and kisses. "Did you think I was making it up?"

"Well, we have a surprise for you," Tina said. "For Mom, too. Kind of a reward."

"You do?" I said.

"It's from all of us," Amber said, putting her arm around my mother.

Jason looked anxious. "You said I could tell them at the party, remember?"

"Aw, let's just tell them," my mother said.

"We better wait," Malvin said.

"Present it properly," Amber agreed.

From the way everybody was smirking, you could tell they'd been planning this—whatever it was—for a long time. I tried to catch Harry's eye, but he was already at the door, staring out into the bright summer morning.

"If we want to get good seats," he said, "we'd better think about leaving pretty soon."

It turned out that Harry was right: The front of the high school's small auditorium was already full by the time we arrived. Amber found us seats about halfway back. We settled into metal folding chairs guaranteed to aggravate lower lumbar complaints.

"Jason *does* look grown-up, doesn't he?" I murmured to Harry as Jason hurried away to review his valedictorian speech.

When Harry didn't reply, I put my hand over his. He glanced at me suddenly, as if I'd surprised him. His face looked wistful. I had to feel sorry for him. He hadn't seen all that much of Jason lately, what with the IPO. How he must regret that now. In less than a week, Jason would leave for his summer program at Stanford. In effect, his childhood would be over. Harry and I would be official Empty Nesters.

"I'm going to stretch my legs a little," Harry said. He got up and wandered away, stopping to chat with other parents and family members, some of whom shook his hand. Once, he would have kept close to me, his arms crossed tightly over his chest, as if he were trying to hide behind them. But Harry wasn't shy the way he used to be before he'd lost weight. Before he'd been promoted at work. Before he'd developed this new, outgoing confidence. Not that there was anything wrong with confidence. My mother, I realized, was whispering to me, her scented hair tickling my cheek.

"What?"

"Aren't you and Harry getting along?"

Because it was my mother asking, I had to answer honestly. "I don't know."

"What do you mean, you don't know?"

I wanted to explain about the IPO, but Harry had made me promise not to tell anybody. "It's just that he's been working so much," I said vaguely.

My mother narrowed her eyes. "Lots of late nights, huh?"

I nodded.

"What about weekends?"

I nodded again.

"Does he seem unusually distracted?"

I tried to laugh. "That isn't just Harry, Mom, that's half the men on the planet!"

"What about . . . ?" She glanced at my hips, then moved her own pelvis suggestively. I looked away, mortified.

"None of your business," I said.

To my surprise, my mother put her hand over mine. "Do you think there's somebody else?"

I jerked my hand away.

"Harry wouldn't—" I began, then stopped. A balloon drifted down from the ceiling of the auditorium; I glanced up and realized that an enormous bag of balloons was up there, waiting for the signal to drop.

"Even if it's true," my mother said, opening her purse and checking her lipstick in a small gold compact, "it's a symptom, not the disease." She applied a fresh blizzard of powder to her nose, then snapped the compact shut with a satisfied sound. "And you have to be practical about these things. Remember what Gracie said after George stepped out on her?"

I managed to shake my head. "Who?"

My mother gave me a look of exaggerated patience. "Gracie Allen? George Burns?"

I was finding it hard to concentrate. It was as if I were coming out of a long spell of amnesia, recognizing my name after months of ignorant bliss.

"After Gracie found out about it, he bought her a fur coat— you know, to help make up. A few years pass and then one day she says to a friend, 'You know, I wish George would have another affair. I need a new coat.'"

"Mom," I said, with every scrap of dignity I could muster. "I don't need a coat."

Jason's valedictorian speech was, by all accounts, extraordinary. But the only words that made any sense to me were the ones my mother had spoken. My trip down *de Nile* was over. My boat had overturned. I was swimming with the piranhas and crocodiles and snakes. Harry, my Harry—how could this have happened? How could I not have seen it? What was I going to do next? By the time Jason had finished speaking, tears were streaming down my cheeks. Fortunately, there were plenty of tears in the auditorium that day, and sad tears don't look any different from happy ones. I blubbered. I bawled. After a while, Harry handed me a handkerchief. It was pale blue, trimmed with satin. I didn't want to blow my nose in anything that pretty.

"Where did you get this?" I managed to say.

"Oh," he said. "Somebody gave it to me."

I stared at it. Something flickered deep inside my brain. My sniveling ceased. "Who?"

The principal was speaking now. Harry shook his head, meaning, *Shh*.

"Who gave it to you?" I spoke clearly. The people ahead of us twisted in their seats, shot me dirty looks.

"Somebody from Group," he said.

The flicker became a steady light, an illuminating beacon that fell on Lucy's business card. I saw that card in exquisite detail: the embossed letters, the gold trim. I recalled Lucy's tailored suit and matching little round purse. Her expensive haircut. Her manicured hands. As the principal nattered on about moral values, I stripped off her jacket. I unbuttoned her blouse. I slid her skirt down over her hips, exposing her silk slip, her Barbie-doll underwear. I walked around her slowly, taking in the small, firm breasts, the flat stomach, the first touch of cellulite dimpling her hips. Finally, I did the unspeakable. I picked up her purse. Her eyes widened with horror as I fumbled with the clasp.

"Was it a gift?" I asked. Never, in the forty-six years I'd walked this earth, had I opened another woman's purse without permission.

"Yes," Harry said. Then: "No." Then: "Why does it matter?"

There they were: handkerchiefs. Blue, with soft silk borders. The scene changed, and I was in a seedy hotel room, neon lights bleeding through the curtains. Lucy dabbed delicately at her eyes while Harry, wearing only a towel, tried to comfort her. *I feel so terrible about this,* she was saying. *What are we going to tell Francie?*

"So it wasn't a gift?"

The first of the graduates were striding across the stage as the school band labored through "Pomp and Circumstance." Or was it the theme from *Star Wars*? With the high-school band, it was sometimes hard to tell.

"I borrowed it, okay?" Harry hissed. "I meant to give it back."

I turned Lucy's purse upside down and scattered its contents across her naked feet.

"Why," I asked, "would you borrow a woman's handkerchief?"

The people in front of us had turned around again. My mother was listening, too. I sensed every cell, every neuron in her body, pulsing and alert. Harry must have, too.

"Can we talk about this later?" he said through gritted teeth.

Mary Elizabeth's name was called. I recognized her face from the picture Jason kept on his desk—a pretty girl, er, woman, with short red hair and a pierced eyebrow. You could tell by the way she walked that she was one tough cookie. You could tell that if Jason ever stepped out on Mary Elizabeth, she'd saw off his balls with a piece of barbed wire.

I blew my nose into the handkerchief as hard as I could, then handed it back to Harry.

"Here you go," I said.

1 2

My mother rode home with Harry and me; Amber and Malvin brought Tina and Trish. Jason was heading over to Mary Elizabeth's house, along with a group of their friends. From there, they'd hop party to party until they landed in our backyard. They'd be there by six-thirty at the latest, Jason promised. Everybody knew that Harry was cooking again. And vegetarian shish kebabs were Mary Elizabeth's favorite.

It was already one-thirty by the time Harry dropped us off.

"Soon as I get these faxes," he began, his voice almost shrill with artificial cheer, but I got out of the car without waiting for him to finish. My mother got out, too. Then she leaned back in.

"Remember, Harry," I heard her say. "At night, all faxes are gray."

At three-thirty, just as I was making the cauliflower salad, the phone rang. Harry, of course. Just calling to say hello, you know. Just hoping everything was okay. Just letting me know he'd be home in, say, half an hour. In the meantime, would I mind soaking the shish kebab skewers in water? And maybe turning the lamb in the marinade a couple of times?

"What about the cake?" I said, each word a block of ice.

"It's under control."

"It better be."

At four o'clock, two hours early, the first of the guests

arrived. I'd just finished tossing the salad. Trish and Tina were chopping cabbage for the coleslaw, and Amber and Malvin were pitting grapes for fruit salad. All of us were drinking my mother's killer screwdrivers, and she'd been whipping up a second batch when an officer of the United States Armed Forces, in full-dress regalia, made his way between the hedgerow dividing our yards. He collapsed noisily into a folding chair, then fanned himself briskly with his cap.

"How about a screw . . . driver?" my mother called out the window.

At the sound of her voice, Mr. Polk fanned harder. "Either or both. Ladies' choice."

My mother and Mr. Polk had started what we all called their flirtation back when Jason was still in grade school. It wasn't surprising, I reflected, that Mr. Polk might show up early. Nor was it surprising when, ten minutes later, Malva appeared as well. But by the time I'd arranged a platter with cold cuts and cheese, Mari and Beth were already setting up the croquet set. Then, stepping outside to say hello, I noticed a white Cadillac listing up the street. Horrified, I watched as it tacked from curb to curb before docking, with a scraping of hubcaps, in front of our house.

Mathilde and Harold Kligler, Sr. Ready or not, the party was under way.

I recruited Malvin to lug out the coolers and fill them with beverages and ice, while I threw together a second platter of vegetables and onion dip. My mother mixed another batch of screwdrivers. By the time Harry called at five to say that the last fax had finally come in, Jason and his friends had arrived.

"Has anybody started the grill?" Harry asked.

I had a yard full of company. It was our son's graduation. It wasn't the time or place to say even one-tenth of the one hundred things I could have said.

"Malvin's on it. Anything else?"

"Did you put out the cold cuts and cheese?"

Done.

"What about the vegetables?"

Ditto.

"I made up some dip. It's in a yellow bowl in the refrig—"

Found it.

"I'm leaving now," Harry said. "I'm sorry, everything's hitting at once, and—"

"Are you at your desk right now?" I asked.

The question seemed to take him by surprise.

"Ye-es."

I squinted at the caller ID box, one of Harry's many gadgets, something I'd insisted that we'd never use. The number in the window was Harry's cell phone number. He might be at his desk. He might be anywhere.

"I'll call you right back," I said.

I hung up before he could say anything, then dialed his office number. After six rings, the office machine picked up. I waited for the beep.

"You're not at your desk," I said.

Like an automaton, I started the grill, slaloming back to the kitchen between the crush of guests on the patio. "Harry's running a little late," I called airily. "No, I don't need help; everything's under control." Amber and Malvin were circulating, arm in arm, like a professional host and hostess. Mr. Polk and my mother had teamed up against Mari and Beth in a brutal game of croquet. Mathilde was loading a plate of cold cuts for Harry Senior. One of Jason's friends had set up a boom box, and I watched for a moment as the kids all danced to Santana. Jason was dancing with Mary Elizabeth, her red hair flashing in the sunlight. He danced the way that Harry danced, a little bit self-consciously. Suddenly, I wondered if I'd ever dance with Harry again. Did Harry take Lucy dancing? Or did they skip such preliminaries altogether? I wondered where they met—her office at the hospital? Our comfy old Taurus? Certainly not the Taurus!

It was five-thirty when Harry burst into the kitchen, holding a big white box. "Who'd have thought people would get here so early?" he said, sliding it onto the counter. "Thanks for covering for me."

"What's in the box?" I said, trying to keep my voice steady.

He began to slice down the sides. "Don't get mad," he said. "I bought a cake."

"Mad's just the tip of the iceberg, Harry."

"Jason won't care. He only eats the frosting, anyway."

"*I* care."

"It isn't your cake, it's Jason's. Could we please not fight about this?"

It was a lemon sheet cake. The frosting was two inches thick, the color of margarine. Across the top, it said YOU GO, GIRL! in lavender script.

"It's hideous," I said.

"It's the last one in Pittsburgh." Harry grabbed a butter knife and began to lift off the Y. "All these graduations. I had to bribe the kid behind the counter into letting me have it." He flipped the Y into the sink, started on the O.

"Harry," I said. "Just admit it."

The sounds of the party washed in through the windows: the warble of conversation, broken by shouts of laughter. The fortune-teller had arrived, and people were lining up to discover what their futures held.

"I bought a cake, I already told you that." He was smoothing the frosting to cover the place where YOU GO, GIRL! had been. "Please, Francie. It's been a really stressful day."

"You're having an affair with her. Don't make me say her name."

He didn't react. He didn't even flinch. Instead, he began slicing the cake into squares—an act that betrayed him completely. Ordinarily, Harry would never have pre-sliced a cake. He'd have sliced as he'd served, so each piece would stay moist.

"You saw her this afternoon," I guessed. "After you picked up your faxes. You've been seeing her after your group meetings. You've been seeing her after work."

The slicing ceased.

"How did you . . ." Harry looked from me to the fortune-teller in the yard. Then he shook his head. "It isn't like that, Francie."

"Tell me what it's not like."

"Nothing has happened. Nothing significant."

"Define 'nothing significant.' "

He lowered his gaze. "I think you know what I mean."

"Do you really expect me to believe you?"

"Yes."

"Why?"

Harry finally raised his eyes. "Because it's true. We've kissed and I'm sorry about that, Francie. I keep telling myself that it's going to stop."

It was strange, but I felt closer to him, at that moment, than I had in weeks. We were having a conversation. We were speaking honestly, face-to-face.

"She looks up to me," Harry said. "She makes me feel—"

Footsteps pounded up the steps, and I heard the screen door opening.

"Dad?" Jason called, coming into the kitchen. He was leading Mary Elizabeth by the hand. "Oh, good! I want you to meet Mary Elizabeth. Mary Elizabeth, this is my mom and dad."

Automatically, instinctively, Harry and I assumed the position. We stood side by side, our faces wreathed in smiles. "We've heard so much about you," Harry said, and I told Mary Elizabeth how lovely it was to meet her after all this time. She nodded as if she'd expected nothing less, ran a brisk hand through her fiery hair. Then her eye fell on the cake. "Oh!" she exclaimed pleasantly. "That's the same kind my parents got. It's from Beckman's Bakery, right?"

Harry's cheeks turned the color of Mary Elizabeth's hair. "I ran out of time on your cake, 'Tart," he said.

Jason laughed. "It doesn't matter. Hey, you want me to start the shish kebabs? I think people are getting hungry."

Harry had been right about one thing: Jason didn't care about the cake.

The shish kebabs were a raving success. So was the coleslaw, the cauliflower salad, the fruit salad. Even the awful cake was admired. Harry and I sat side by side, across from Mathilde and Harry Senior, who between them put away roughly two dozen shish kebabs. Harry Junior, I noticed, seemed to have lost his appetite. I, on the other hand, cleaned my plate. I made it through several more of my mother's screwdrivers as well. I talked and joked with Malva. I praised Jason's teachers, chatted with Mary Elizabeth. This, I realized, was the easy part. After fearing the worst, the worst had come. My marriage was over. I would have to sell the house. I'd wind up renting a small apartment in a seedy section of town. I'd pass my days reading articles that described my chances of falling in love again as slightly less than being hijacked.

I realized that everybody had fallen silent. Jason stood at the head of the table; Amber floated between the guests, pouring champagne. Citronella candles flickered and danced in the growing dusk.

"First of all," Jason said, "I'd like to thank everybody for coming to my graduation party. But, as we all know, that isn't the only thing we have to celebrate."

I looked around. Amber and Malvin were smiling at Harry and me in a knowing way. So were the twins. Only my mother looked less than delighted. She was, I realized, looking daggers at Harry.

Now I understood. We were about to get our anniversary gift.

"It's an accomplishment to graduate from high school," Jason said. "But it's a rare accomplishment to stay married for twenty-five years. And it's also truly inspiring, I mean, for us kids"—he faltered a little, swallowed hard with emotion—"to have such a great example of what a marriage can be. Some of you may have noticed that my dad seems to be shrinking."

There was laughter and applause. Harry's smile looked as if it had been carved into his face.

"It takes a lot of willpower and determination to change your life, but my dad did it. He did it for us. He did it for my mom." Jason shot me a look of pure boyish adoration. "But he wouldn't have been able to do it *without* my mom."

All around me, heads were bobbing.

"Since January first, my mom has done all the cooking, and all the shopping, which I guess makes her like a lot of other moms." Jason glanced nervously at Mary Elizabeth. When she did not appear to object, he continued. "But my mom learned to cook in a whole new way. She learned how to make foods that Dad could eat. She also took over a lot of other things, I mean, around the house, and with us kids . . ." He faltered again. "Well, she made time for Dad to go to the gym and develop new interests and, well, be away from home a lot more than we've all been used to."

Harry passed his hands over his face.

"So that's why all of us kids plus Grandma Sylvia and Grampa and Grandma Kligler have chipped in to give both Mom and Dad something we hope they'll remember for the rest of their lives." He dug around in the pockets of his suit coat. He dug some more. Eventually, Malvin—smirking a little—handed him an envelope.

Everybody laughed.

"Thanks," Jason said, visibly relieved. "Mom, Dad, Happy Anniversary. Here's to the next twenty-five years."

Glasses of champagne were pushed into our hands. I seemed to be holding an envelope. I looked at Harry, at the envelope, at Harry. What I really wanted was another screwdriver. Would anybody notice if I got up to look for the pitcher?

"Open it," Harry said hoarsely.

I obeyed. Inside was an itinerary. I skimmed the information. One week from today, on the morning of June 25, we'd fly to

Miami. Later that same afternoon, we'd board the luxury cruise ship *Czarina* for a one-week low-carbohydrate gourmet cruise. All cuisine would be prepared by the finest international chefs. Ports of call would include San Juan and St. Thomas. I opened the glossy brochure.

Couples lounging by a pool, waving spicy chicken wings. Had I seen this brochure before?

"It's only a week," Amber said, "and we know you've both got two weeks' vacation. But you've been so busy, we thought it would be better to leave the second week unscheduled. You could rent a car and go to the Keys or something. Or you could just come home and sleep."

"Do you like it?" Jason said.

Everybody waited. Harry and I exchanged glances, then rose to our feet.

"We love it," Harry said. "Especially since we've been too busy to make solid plans ourselves."

"This is perfect," I said. "Thank you. Thank you, every-body."

Somebody started banging their fork against their cham-pagne glass. Lightly at first. Soon the sound spread, glass to glass, rising into the darkening air.

"Kiss the bride!" Mr. Polk shouted.

"Kiss the bride!" Malva picked up the cry.

"Kiss the bride! Kiss the bride!"

There was no help for it. I tried to remember the last time we'd kissed. I tried to remember *how* to kiss. But when Harry's lips met mine, it all came back. I kissed him long and hard—or maybe he kissed me. We kissed as if we were having a long and private conversation, one that was painful, but full of truth. We kissed as if our tongues were swords and we wanted to kill each other. We kissed as if we really were newlyweds, our lives just beginning, the idea that either of us would ever want anything else as incomprehensible as the speed of light. We kissed until people stopped banging on their glasses and started laughing, and then stopped laughing and stared at us uncomfortably.

Then, one by one, they started kissing, too. The kissing spread couple to couple, table to table, the way that the sound of tinkling glassware had spread, so that when Harry and I finally broke apart, we saw a tangle of arms and faces: Amber and Malvin, Mari and Beth, Jason and Mary Elizabeth. My mother and Mr. Polk. Two of Jason's teachers were kissing.

Gradually, people recalled themselves. Jason and his friends decided it was time to move along to their next party. Harry Senior and Mathilde checked their watches. Mr. Polk and my mother slunk off through the hedgerow. Within a matter of minutes, it seemed, the party had ended. Pricked. Deflated. Those kisses had done it. They'd been too sharp. They'd punctured the atmosphere like a balloon.

Harry and I stood at the end of the driveway, saying our good-byes as the twins cleared the tables, as Malvin collapsed and stacked the chairs. Inside, Amber was cleaning up the kitchen. Mari and Beth had already hauled the trash out to the curb. As soon as the last of the guests were gone, there'd be nothing more for Harry and me to do—aside from saying good-bye to the twins, who had an early flight back to Vermont. We'd hug them and kiss them. We'd hug and kiss Amber and Malvin, too. We'd stand in the driveway one more time, waving until the lights of the Mercedes had disappeared altogether. Then we'd pour ourselves a nightcap—single malt scotch for Harry, white wine for me—and sit on the patio. We'd watch the fireflies, listen to the crickets. We'd dissect the evening, discuss every detail, just the way we'd always done after one of Harry's neighborhood dinners.

And that was exactly what we did. It couldn't have been more natural. Sitting on the patio, we shook our heads over my mother and Mr. Polk, pictured my mother living next door. (Don't even joke about it, Harry said.) We talked about Tina and Trish, who, it seemed, were content with the life they'd made together. We wondered if Malvin and Amber would ever marry. If Jason and Mary Elizabeth would last. If everybody had enjoyed themselves tonight—but of course they had. It had been a wonderful party. Everybody had come. Well, almost everybody.

"I was sorry that Krys and the girls didn't make it," I said, taking a sip of my wine.

Quick as an eye-blink, the night changed. The air seemed too still, too silent. The stars glimmered unwholesomely.

"You are?" Harry's voice was dry.

"Well, yes," I said, speaking a little too loudly, trying to fill the void. "I haven't seen Krys since Amber remodeled the den. What a day that was!" I was hoping to rekindle our earlier intimacy.

But there was only more silence. I could hear Harry swallowing. Finally he spoke.

"I think it would have been awkward," he said. "Under the circumstances."

What circumstances? I almost said it. Then the earth began to buckle and shift; the air filled with sound once more. The stars roared with laughter. The crickets jeered.

"You were with Krys this afternoon," I said.

Harry stared at me. "You said you knew."

I repeated: "With Krys."

"She had a bad phone call from John. She had no one else to talk to."

"*Krys.*"

"I don't understand," Harry said, his voice rising. "Who else, I mean, who did you think—?"

In my mind's eye, I saw poor, naked Lucy give me the finger.

"It doesn't matter," I said.

For a moment, neither one of us said anything.

"Do you want a divorce?" I asked the question pleasantly, the way I might have asked if he wanted a cup of coffee. "Do you want to throw away twenty-five years?"

"Francie," he said. "Stop."

But all those screwdrivers had loosened my tongue. "You want to move in with her? I'll help you pack. Hell, I'll help you pack tonight."

"It isn't that simple."

"Sure it is." I took a gulp of wine. "Here are your choices. You want to leave? Go. You want to stay? We walk across the street and knock on Krys's door, and we tell her in no uncertain terms that nothing, either significant or insignificant, is ever going to happen between you two again."

I allowed him a five-count beat of silence before I stood.

"Time's up," I said.

"I need to tell you something," Harry said.

"That isn't one of your choices." Suddenly I was very, very tired—so tired that I had to sit back down again. I figured that whatever he was about to say was something I didn't want to know. That he'd lied and he'd already slept with her. That there was no IPO, no VCs, no B2B software. That all those nights I'd believed him to be at the gym, he'd actually been with Krys, conjugating Polish verbs.

But—

"I love you," he said. "Do you still love me?"

I wanted to cry. "Yes," I said. *"Yes."* The past few months hadn't been so great. All right, they'd been awful. But weighed against the good years, the sweet times—well, what were a few sour months? "So if we love each other," I said, "what is all this about?"

"I'm not sure," Harry said. "I need time to figure it out. I wish I could just get away from everything for a while."

"In another ten days, we'll be in St. Thomas. That's about as far away from everything as you can get."

Too late, I realized he'd said *I* instead of *we.*

"I can't go to St. Thomas," Harry said.

I stared at him. "What?"

"The timing couldn't be worse. That meeting tomorrow? It's the last big hurdle. After that, it's all systems go for the IPO."

"You're canceling our vacation? It's our twenty-fifth anniversary."

"I'm sorry, Francie," Harry said. "I can't go."

"You mean you *won't* go."

Harry didn't say anything.

"Well, *I'm* going. You see, I happen to be free. I've had those two weeks marked on my calendar for the past year."

Harry bowed his head. "Maybe that's not a bad idea, taking some time for yourself. I'm going to be working around the clock for the next few weeks, anyway."

Now I understood. When he'd said that he wanted to get

away from everything, what he'd meant was that he wanted to get away from me.

"And will Krys be working around the clock, too?"

"That's not what this is about."

"Only a big part of it."

I stood up and tossed what was left of my wine at the man I'd loved for more than twenty-five years. He didn't flinch. He'd been expecting it.

"You want a vacation from me, from this marriage?" I said. "Fine. But in that case, Harry, I'm entitled to a little vacation of my own."

13

We boarded an early-morning flight to Miami on the first of July. By mid-afternoon, we were sitting in the limousine Amber had arranged, cruising in air-conditioned comfort toward the harbor where the two-thousand-passenger *Czarina* floated high on the water like a big, white wedding cake. I'd imagined the "staterooms" as closet-sized cells, each with a single round portal for light. But the white-gloved attendant carrying our bags unlocked the door to a majestic suite. There was a king-sized bed, a plush couch and chair, a large TV, and a wet bar. A table stood before sliding glass doors that opened onto a balcony. On the table were fresh-cut flowers, a bottle of chilled champagne. I opened the card attached to the flowers.

Happy 25th Anniversary! read a stranger's hand. It was signed, *Your captain and crew*.

The kids had thought of everything.

"I wonder if there's any more news about the weather," Tommy said, coming out of the bathroom.

I had a momentary flicker of guilt. I doused the flame with an image of Harry moving into Krys's house while I was away. It was odd seeing Tommy in shorts; I tried not to stare at his legs. Then I remembered they were mine to stare at—at least for the next six days.

Tommy said, "Mind if I turn on the TV?"

We were being extra-polite with each other. We were like teenagers on a first date: trying to look casual, nervous as hell.

"No, I don't mind," I said.

Let me say here that I hadn't meant to end up on a cruise with Tommy Choi. Originally, I'd intended to invite Lindy to use Harry's ticket. Max owed her big for the week he'd spent skiing, leaving her to wrestle with Raymond all alone, and I felt certain she'd be delighted to exchange a week at the Jersey Shore for a tropical cruise—and for only the price of a change fee. And yet I didn't call her. I couldn't admit to anyone, yet, that my marriage was falling apart. I avoided my mother's phone calls. Mornings, Harry and I moved around the kitchen like strangers, excusing ourselves if our shoulders happened to touch. Nights, we slept at opposite corners of the bed. We managed to keep up appearances until Jason left for Stanford, putting him on the plane with enormous smiles on our faces. Then, as soon as we got home, Harry moved into the twins' room. Late at night, I could hear him talking on his cell phone. It might have been Krys. It might have been one of the dot-cowboys. I didn't know what to believe anymore. The big board meeting, it turned out, had been real. The IPO was moving forward. The few times I did call Harry at work, he was always at his desk.

"You don't need to keep checking up on me."

"I'm not checking up on you. I just wanted to talk."

"Can we talk later? I have a meeting in five minutes."

"Are you in love with her?"

"Francie, I'm at work, okay? This isn't helping either of us."

He had a point. The attempts we made at talking inevitably deteriorated into fighting. A vacation from all that—a cooling-off period—was beginning to look better and better.

The night before my flight to Miami, I'd stayed late at the clinic to clear my desk. It was a Friday night. The halls were silent. I opened the first fat insurance file, took a swig of coffee, and dug in. But after an hour, I realized it was hopeless. How Harry could bury himself in work at a time like this was beyond me. I couldn't concentrate for more than a minute before my thoughts were wandering again. Maybe I was making a strategic mistake, leaving him alone with Krys for a week. But if he *was* truly falling in love with someone else, it would happen whether or not I was around. This was, as far as I could tell, the first time in twenty-five years that another woman had looked his way. It didn't say much for him that he'd been so easily tempted. And even if this particular infatuation passed, there would be others as Harry lost more weight. As he rose in importance at his company. Suddenly, it truly hit me: My marriage was over. Life as I'd known it was over.

My head ached. Bleary-eyed with tears, I packed up my things, went out to the parking lot, and got into our big old lumbering Taurus. I glanced in the rearview mirror, saw nothing. I put the Taurus in reverse. I'd only meant to tap the gas, but somehow the Taurus squealed back with a lurch—

—smashing full tilt into Tommy's Lexus, which just happened to be gliding past.

As soon as I heard the terrible crunch of metal upon metal, my headache vanished. I understood everything now. I'd killed my friend Tommy. I was about to go to jail. At least I didn't need to worry about the future anymore.

I watched in the rearview mirror as a figure emerged from the wreckage. Light poured down upon him from the tall steel lamp in the center of the lot. He looked like an angel. He hovered just above the asphalt. When he put his face close to my window, I stared as if he were someone I'd never seen before.

"Are you okay?" he said.

I nodded. Now I knew he was an angel. Any other living human male would have cussed me out.

I climbed out of the car and into his arms. He didn't act altogether unhappy about this. I would have been quite content to stay there and let him rub my shoulders, but after a moment, he said, "Uh, Fran? Maybe we better call the police."

It took over an hour for the police to arrive. It took half an hour more to do the paperwork. By that time, Tommy knew all about Krys and Harry, and I knew that Tommy—unable to bear his empty house—had been sleeping on the couch in his office. He'd been borrowing sheets and blankets from the linen closets. Mornings, he showered in the therapy room. He said it really wasn't that bad. In fact, he'd just been heading out to re-stock his mini-fridge when I inflicted eight thousand dollars' worth of damage on his vehicle.

The Taurus, of course, was just fine.

The tow truck arrived. The tow truck left. Perhaps, Tommy said, I would be so good as to give him a lift to the store? Unless Harry was waiting for me.

I knew, without a shadow of a doubt, that Harry was not waiting for me. I burst into tears again.

Tommy thought that maybe we ought to pick up a six-pack, too.

Back in his office, we sat on opposite ends of the couch,

clutching our sweating beers as the bust of Robert Frost glow-
ered down at us. Tommy explained that Robert Frost was the
most misunderstood poet in America. He quoted a Robert
Frost poem about a daffodil. He ranted against contemporary
critics—revisionists, he called them—who dared to assert that
Frost had been a bigot, a misogynist, a violent man. "Literary
theorists," he said, rolling his eyes. I had no idea what he was
talking about, but I rolled my eyes, too. The next thing I knew,
Tommy was kissing me passionately. Or maybe I was kissing
him. It was really hard to tell.

At first, Tommy had had reservations about accompanying
me on a cruise purchased by my children for my twenty-fifth
wedding anniversary. On the other hand, he acknowledged
that, given the state of things with Jessica, mine was the only
twenty-fifth wedding anniversary he was likely to celebrate. I
suggested another beer might help him sort things through.
Another beer, another round of soul kisses, and Tommy
allowed as how he thought the cruise was an excellent idea. It
wouldn't be wise, after all, for him to return straight to work
after a traumatic accident like the one he'd just experienced.
Symptoms could take several days to appear. One couldn't be
too careful. In fact, come to think of it, his neck was feeling
rather stiff. He'd better take the week off.

And so here we sat, side by side at the foot of a king-sized
bed, watching the distant, fading swirl of a tropical storm
named Dolores. I could feel the weight of his body next to
mine. I could smell his shampoo, a faint whisper of deodorant,
and something else, something warm and male and pleasing
that was nothing like the way Harry smelled. Harry's smell was
muskier, lightened by sweet traces of aftershave. After he show-

ered, I liked to press my nose against the base of his neck, and—

I killed the thought by imagining what Krys smelled like.

"Poor downgraded Dolores," Tommy said. "She isn't even a tropical storm anymore."

"We're lucky," I said.

"Yes, we are."

I leaned over and kissed him. His tongue played over mine. I thought of Arnie Grant's long-ago kisses. I thought of the long afternoons Harry and I had spent in his dorm room under the ceiling of flags. I thought of Jessica, and it crossed my mind that she must be crazy to give up a wonderful man like Tommy, as crazy as Harry was for giving up a wonderful woman like me. Harry—there he was again. He was rolling around with Krys on a king-sized bed just like this one. I gasped.

"Sorry," Tommy said, pulling back.

"No," I said, putting my hand to my mouth. "I'm fine. I—"

One by one, Tommy peeled my fingers back, revealing my mouth like a piece of fruit. He moved so slowly, so deliberately, so . . . *delectably*. I felt like a movie star. I felt like an adulterer. When he kissed me again, my stomach sank deep into my groin, where his kisses and Harry's kisses got tangled up together in a weirdly pornographic kind of way. I wondered if Harry had felt the same way the first time he kissed Krys. Tommy took my face in his hands as if it were something he wanted to eat.

"Don't take this wrong," I murmured. "But I keep seeing Harry in my head."

"What's he doing?" Tommy kissed my eyes, one by one.

"You don't want to know," I said.

Tommy pressed his forehead to mine. "Jessica is writing in her journal," he said. "She's sitting in the middle of her big white couch and she's sipping a glass of white wine. The apartment is absolutely quiet. Except . . ." He genuinely seemed to be listening. "Except for a Mozart piano concerto."

"That's it?" I said.

He nodded.

"That doesn't seem too bad," I said.

"Did I mention," he said, "that I'm the last thing on her mind?"

Now I understood.

"Look," he said. "We've both been rejected, right? So let's enjoy being chosen for a change."

He kissed me lightly on the forehead. He kissed me lightly on the ear. He kissed my throat and I lifted my hands to his hair, soft and thick and shining. Gently, he pushed me back onto the bed. I closed my eyes, letting his mouth work its way down my shirt, button by button. I arched my back so he could unhook my bra, and he was doing something delicious with his tongue when it seemed as if we were tossed into the air, borne on a solid wave of sound that rose from somewhere deep within the ship's belly. Both of us yelped, before collapsing in a fit of giggles. The ship's horn sounded again, so loud and full it made my fillings ache.

The *Czarina* was under way.

Tommy pulled me to my feet, and I scrambled after him onto the balcony, holding my shirt closed with one hand. The dock was lined with people. Everyone was waving. Tommy waved back, and as I felt the ship move beneath us, I thought of Harry's face at the moment when I told him I'd be flying to Miami with Tommy.

"You're joking," he said.

"Do I look like I'm joking?"

"But he's *married,* Francie. Think about what you're doing."

"Actually, he's separated. You and I are married, remember?"

The last of my doubts vanished along with the Miami skyline. We were heading out into open seas.

"Let's open the champagne," I said.

∗   ∗   ∗

I HAD NEVER been on a cruise before. Tommy had, once, with Jessica, but he said he didn't remember it too well, because he'd spent most of it curled up in a little green ball on the bathroom floor. There had been a storm, and though it lasted only a day, the high seas continued for most of the trip. The ship's store ran out of Dramamine. The dance floors stayed empty, the buffet tables untouched.

"It was nothing like this, believe me," Tommy said.

We had eaten, and now we were dancing, and soon we would be eating again. The food was exquisite: lobster tails, avocado halves piled with crabmeat, shrimp twice the size of my thumb. There were low-carb fruit cocktails made with grape-sized blueberries and raspberries; there were crème brûlées and mousses that slid down your throat like satin. It had taken us several hours to explore the entire ship—swimming pools and casinos, coffee shops and piano bars, gift shops and art galleries—before we'd reached the upper ballroom.

There, a dance band called Protein Power was belting out all the old favorites. The dress code was "Cruise Casual," which seemed to mean everything from sundresses and cutoffs to off-the-shoulder designer gowns. Tommy, of course, wore his Birkenstocks. I was wearing open-backed pumps and a flowery cotton dress. Many of the dancers had opted for gift shop T-shirts with slogans like I'M A LOSER! and THIS BABY RUNS ON PROTEIN!

A tall, thin gentleman danced into me, stepped back, apologized. "How much did you lose?" he asked, shouting to be heard over the band.

"Forty pounds!" I lied.

"Congratulations! You?" He looked at Tommy.

"Twenty!"

"Two hundred," he hollered, thumping his belly.

"Congratulations!" we said.

Already we were learning the native tongue. Tommy pulled me close. "I'm getting one of those loser T-shirts to wear to my divorce hearing," he said into my ear.

How long had it been since I'd heard the Village People? When had I last danced to "Rock Lobster"? Bullets of light drizzled down from the crystal chandelier as we all melted onto the floor. It shifted beneath us, and for the first time since we'd started dancing, I remembered that we were somewhere in the middle of the Atlantic, not in the heart of Times Square. I stumbled and Tommy caught me firmly.

"I could do with some water," I said.

"Me, too."

As the band struck up a reggae version of "You Don't Bring Me Flowers," we wove our way over to the bar. I could definitely feel the ship's motion. It wasn't unpleasant, but it had been a while since I'd last worn pumps. I braced myself against the wall while Tommy got our drinks. The beverage selection was odd. You could get a Perrier, or an Evian, or a double scotch on the rocks—but no wine or beer.

Too many carbs.

Tommy came back with some kind of imported water infused with an essence of peach. It was heavenly. We hugged our wall, watched the dancing couples. Some appeared to be holding each other in a way that seemed more functional than romantic. A man walking past lurched forward, sloshing his drink across the floor.

"Feeling some waves," Tommy observed. "Is it hot in here, or is it just me?"

"Sweltering. Want to cool off outside?"

"We could walk around the upper deck, look at the moon." He linked his arm through mine.

I imagined the sound of the waves, the brightness of the stars against the sky. The cool breeze lifting my hair. Tommy's mouth over mine. I saw the king-sized bed in our stateroom, the covers turned down, inviting. I felt a strange sense of hyper-reality. I was going to make love with a man who wasn't Harry.

I couldn't wait.

We left the ballroom and hurried down the corridor until we reached the stairs leading up onto the outer deck. But the doors were locked. A ship's mate stepped forward, elegant in his white uniform.

"I apologize," he said, in the voice of a waiter who has just run out of the house special. "There's a little bit of weather. The captain wants everyone to stay inside."

The ship swayed obligingly, as if to prove his point. I teetered on my pumps. "What does that mean, a little bit of weather?"

"Nothing to worry about," the mate said in that same even voice. "We're changing course to avoid the worst of her."

"Her?" Tommy looked anxious. "You mean Dolores? I thought she was downgraded."

By now, a few other couples had bunched up behind us. The ship swayed again. Somebody stepped on the back of my heel, and I heard a mumbled "Sorry!"

"Well, she's picked up again," the mate said. "But she's heading northeast and we're already south of her. We'll feel her tonight for a while, but by morning . . ."

He paused. There was an oddly magnified sound, a kind of whistle that reverberated through the corridors.

"That's the captain," he said. He sounded relieved. "He'll be making a general announcement."

Again, the whistle blew, and a mechanized voice said, *Attention! Attention!* Then came the voice of the real, live captain. He, too, sounded like a waiter who'd just run out of the house special. Only he sounded even more regretful, as if the house special had been, alas, the only dish on the menu worth ordering. He requested everyone's attention and cooperation. Mother Nature had surprised the meteorologists with a bit of unseasonable weather. For our safety and comfort, he was going to suspend the rest of the evening's activities. We were asked to return to our staterooms and remain there. He recommended that we all turn in for the night.

"This is not good," Tommy said as we turned back toward

the bank of elevators that would take us to our deck. I stopped
to slip off my pumps; other women were doing the same. The
doors of the ballroom were open now, and sweaty dancers
poured down the passageways. Suddenly there seemed to be
uniformed crew members everywhere, politely but firmly moving us along.

"It doesn't seem that bad," I said, bending my knees to
absorb the next roll. Ahead of me, a man fell forward and was
caught by two laughing women. Strangers held on to one
another; couples giggled as they knocked knees and hips.
Everything seemed to be swaying, and for some reason, this
was hilarious. The only person who seemed immune to this
general giddiness was Tommy.

"Just you wait," he said.

By the time we reached our corridor, I was feeling a bit like
a pinball rolling through a maze. My hip bumped a fire extin-
guisher: ten points. My elbow flew into Tommy's side: twenty.
Just as we reached our room, the ship rose—a delightful, airy
feeling—and when it rolled back down and down and down,
we fell into each other's arms: jackpot. Only Tommy wasn't
looking like he'd won anything.

"I've got scopolamine patches in my bag," he said, breaking
free to unlock the door to our stateroom.

"Patches?"

Tommy had the door open. "You stick them behind your
ear. They help prevent seasickness."

"Do you feel sick?"

He didn't answer. Perhaps he hadn't heard me.

I sat down on the bed and watched him dig through the
pockets of his garment bag. The ship was definitely rolling

now, a steady rise and fall, as if it were breathing. I lay back. I kind of liked the feeling. It was like being rocked in a giant cradle.

"I feel perfectly fine," I said. "I don't think I need to take anything."

Tommy held up a piece of paper, peeled off a translucent half-moon, and pressed it behind his ear.

"I don't know how much good they'll do," he said. "You need to put them on well in advance. I almost put one on this morning, but they make me sleepy, so I figured I'd risk it." He laughed unhappily as he peeled off another half-moon. "Here, I'll put yours on for you. Don't touch, it can get into your eyes."

"I don't know," I said.

"You'll thank me for this, I promise."

His hands were all business as he pressed it behind my ear.

"I'm going to wash up. You want to turn on the TV? We might be able to see a weather report or something."

I grabbed the remote, but all I got was a screen full of static. Something major must be interfering with the satellite, I thought. Something like a tropical storm. I got up and staggered toward the balcony, but I could see nothing beyond the rail. Beads of water dotted the glass. The carpet was wet beneath my feet, and I looked down to see a scattering of flowers, the vase rolling back and forth along the wall. I picked it up and put it in the nightstand drawer, where it rattled like a small caged animal. Odd that the framed pictures on the walls were perfectly still. I reached out to touch one. It hadn't been hung so much as affixed. Everything in the room, in fact, seemed to be locked down.

I bent to collect the flowers. Orchids. I hated to see them die of thirst. Maybe I could put them in the sink. I gathered them up and went to the bathroom, knocked gently on the door.

"I'll be right out." Tommy's voice sounded pinched. Strained.

The room tilted again, and I let gravity carry me back toward the bed, where it occurred to me that the flowers added a rather romantic touch. I laid one on each of the pillows, spread the remainder across the sheets. What was taking Tommy so long? Maybe he was getting undressed. Maybe I ought to get undressed, too. I tottered in the direction of the luggage rack but was forced to stumble backward as it suddenly pitched forward, sending my suitcase sliding across the floor. I chased it down, dug out my black satin nightie, and scrambled into it as fast as I could. Then I flung myself back on the bed.

There. I was ready. I had nothing to do but wait for Tommy to come out of the bathroom. But all that came out of the bathroom was a sound I instantly recognized, a sound I could not help but feel in the pit of my own stomach. For such a small man, Tommy made a truly extraordinary amount of noise. After a while it stopped.

I got up, knocked on the mirrored door.

"Are you okay?" I asked my reflection.

The response was another, louder, longer series of retches, followed by vigorous nose-blowing. I studied myself, a woman dressed for romance, one black satin strap slipping suggestively off my shoulder. It was impossible to reconcile what I saw with what I heard.

I knocked again. "Can I get you anything?"

"Cyanide," came the response.

I opened the door. Tommy was sitting on the bathroom floor, his back against the shower stall, his skin as pale as my own. Beads of sweat stood out on his forehead, and as I wet a washcloth with cool water, I noticed that the scopolamine patch had slid halfway down his neck. I flicked it away with my fingernail before handing him the washcloth.

"Thanks," he said, wiping his face. A smile flickered across his white, white lips. "I'm having the strangest sense of déjà vu. When you knocked on the door, I thought you were Jessica. I thought it was twenty years ago. Remember I told you we went on a cruise?"

The towels were swaying on their racks. I closed the toilet lid and sat.

"I'd just finished my first year as a resident, and I had a little time off. Jessica's mother worked for a travel agency, and she talked us into a three-day cruise out of Cancún."

He gave a moist little hiccup.

"Want me to move?"

"Not yet." He passed the washcloth over his face, and I had a little déjà vu of my own, remembering nights sitting up with the children, holding their heads over the toilet bowl. "So our first night out, the seas get rough, and *God* . . ." He hiccuped again. "There's a point where you get so sick that everything else falls away, and you see your life for what it really is. No illusions. Only what's there. Everything perfectly clear."

He rolled to his knees. "Now I need you to move."

I leaped out of the way, busied myself with wetting another washcloth.

"I realized," he said when he'd finished, "that I didn't want to be a doctor. That I'd *never* wanted to be a doctor. It was what my parents had wanted. What *I* wanted was to be a poet. And a teacher. And it wasn't too late. I was only twenty-five. I could go back to school. I could start over. I was so very sick that it seemed I could do anything I wanted." He smiled ruefully. "So anyway, I tell Jessica this. She's puking her guts out, too. I say that all I've ever really wanted to do was write poetry. And you know what she says?"

I shook my head. The motion made me dizzy. I thought about sitting down again but then decided against it.

"She says," he panted, "all she ever wanted to do was marry a doctor."

I put my hand on his shoulder. He was sopping with sweat. I was sweating myself.

"You would think," he said, "I'd have had the sense to figure things out then and there."

I wanted to be supportive, but I was finding it hard to concentrate. I slid to my knees beside him.

"I don't feel so good," I said.

❋   ❋   ❋

LATER, MUCH LATER, we'd learn that the *Czarina* had been out of radio contact for almost half an hour. Our captain, hoping to beat the storm, had miscalculated and taken us directly into it. We ended up coming into port at St. Thomas after three days on the high seas. Tommy and I, along with several hundred others, were hospitalized for dehydration, and because the hospital was already overflowing, we ended up assigned to mattresses laid out in the corridors. Twenty-four hours after that, we were sleeping on the floor again, this time at the airport, where we found ourselves stranded along with thousands of other travelers. By this time, we'd stopped speaking. Having seen it all, there was nothing left to say. We were like very old people who have survived a civil war, or a plague. We squinted and blinked at the unfamiliar sunlight. When we walked, we shuffled our feet.

Late in the afternoon of the second day, we were told that flights had been found for each of us—separate flights. Tommy would go home via St. Louis; I would go through Detroit. It didn't matter. Traveling together just didn't seem that important anymore. Tommy's flight left first, and as I hugged him good-bye, I could feel his body trembling—or was it mine? Neither of us had been able to eat. We clutched our stomach muscles when we moved. At least we didn't have to worry about carrying heavy bags. Our luggage had been stolen at the hospital.

"Are you going to be okay?" I asked.

"Are you?" Tommy said.

We kissed like brother and sister.

Many, many hours after that, as I sat in the airport in Detroit, listening to the agent announce the cancellation of my flight, I began to connect the feeling in my stomach to something more than nausea. Something more than exhaustion. Something more than the persistent memory of endless lunges at the toilet. I realized that Tommy had been right: If you got sick enough, miserable enough, desperate enough, you reached a point of absolute clarity. A place where all illusions fell away. The simple truth was this: I wanted to be home. I wanted to be home so badly that my very soul ached with longing. And the home that I still wanted—for better or worse, for richer or poorer—was the home that I'd had with Harry, the home I suddenly understood was worthy of repair at any cost.

Somehow I'd find a way—we'd find a way—to rebuild what we'd lost. I didn't care how long that might take. I would be like the refugee I was now. I would sit in the midst of the wreckage and despair with the face of a very old woman. I would wait, and I would wait, and I would wait longer still, until a ticket was issued, a passage was bought, until some way was found to get me home.

*H*ouses have expressions, just like people do. And there's always a certain look on the face of a house where something inside has gone wrong.

That was the look I expected to see as the taxicab pulled onto our street. It was one in the morning. The air was clear and still. I'd imagined that the house would be dark, the grass overgrown. Raccoons would have overturned the trash; newspapers would be piling up on the porch. I'd feel the chill of the empty rooms even before I opened the door, and once inside, there'd be that stale, faintly rancid smell. Milk gone sour in the refrigerator. Garbage festering underneath the sink.

But cresting the hill, I saw that the lawn was neatly mowed, the garbage cans stacked. Malva, I thought, must have kept an eye on the place. Or Amber. It wasn't that she still had her key so much as that she'd never actually given it up.

A faint light glowed from the back of the house.

When I got out of the cab, a man appeared in the front window, cupped his hand to the glass. With a start, I realized it was Harry. How could I have forgotten that he'd lost so much weight? It crossed my mind that he wasn't expecting to see me any more than I was expecting to see him. What if Krys was there, too? I wasn't sure what to do. Should I ring the bell? Should I just walk in?

I probably would have stood there quite awhile if Harry hadn't opened the door.

"You're back!" he said, and then, "Come in," and then, "I mean, of course, come in, you live here, right?"

"Are you alone?" I asked, stepping cautiously inside. I feared that I looked and smelled like someone who'd been sleeping in an airport. It wasn't the look and smell I'd have chosen for greeting my husband's lover.

"Alone?" Harry seemed surprised. "Oh. Yes. I was just watching TV." I walked past him to the kitchen and he followed me. I wanted us to be together in the kitchen. It seemed cozy and familiar.

"Not working?" I put my purse down on the counter and looked around, trying to put my finger on what, exactly, was different.

"Believe it or not, I took the last few days off."

He was watching me expectantly. I looked from the shining countertops to the scoured stove to the sparkling floor. The flour canisters had been polished. The coffeemaker had been cleaned. This was not the state in which I'd left the kitchen only a week earlier.

"You were cooking," I said.

He nodded.

I opened the refrigerator, blinked. He had shopped as well. The shelves were full. There were fresh vegetables. There were Tupperware containers, neatly stacked. Could all this be for me? But no. He'd probably had Krys over for dinner.

"Leftovers?" I said.

"Experiments," he said. "I've been playing around with some low-carb recipes. I don't suppose you're hungry?"

I *was* hungry, actually. A genuine, healthy hunger. I also needed to go to the bathroom, to shower, to sleep for the next ten days.

"Give me fifteen minutes," Harry said. "I'll fix you up a plate."

In the upstairs bathroom, I braced myself before looking in the mirror. To my surprise, I didn't look half-bad. In Detroit, in the rest room, I'd washed my hair with antibacterial hand soap and blasted it dry with the air-dryer. It had turned out better than you'd think. And I'd gotten some sun that first afternoon, drinking champagne with Tommy on the balcony. Tommy. I wondered if he'd made it home. I wondered if I should call him. I couldn't picture his face without feeling an associative twinge of nausea, and I suspected he felt the same way about me. I hopped into the shower, grabbed the loofah, tried to scrub away the bathroom floor, the hospital, the airport.

Harry was waiting for me in the living room. He'd arranged a plate with pecan chicken salad over fanned Granny Smith apple slices. Hard-boiled eggs stuffed with crab. A handful of strawberries. A slice of—what was this?

"Strawberry-rhubarb kuchen," Harry said. "It isn't low-carb, exactly, but it's reduced. I worked on the recipe all afternoon."

The plate was on the coffee table. The coffee table stood in front of the couch, where Harry was already seated. It would have been awkward if I hadn't sat beside him.

"I need to ask you something," I said. "Now that we've had some time apart, I'm wondering how things stand with you and Krys."

I pronounced her name without the slightest trace of resentment. I'd made up my mind to stay calm. This was one conversation that was not going to dissolve into yet another meaningless quarrel.

"Krys?" To my surprise, Harry blushed. I'd forgotten what a blusher he was. I'd forgotten his nicely sloping shoulders, his boyish lower lip, his well-shaped hands. "Actually, I was supposed to see her the night after you left. To talk about, you know, where we were going with all this."

His cheeks were positively flaming now. I prepared myself for the worst.

"I suppose you can guess what happened," he said.

I shook my head.

He smiled ruefully. "Things got crazy at work. I had to stand her up."

I laughed, I couldn't help it.

"I guess she didn't take it very well," Harry continued, "because she called John and told him I was coming on to her."

"Really?"

"Long story short, they're back together again."

I wanted to jump up and down. I wanted to slap the universe a big high five. But I managed to control myself.

"I'm sorry," was all I said.

"You are?" To my amazement, he sounded disappointed.

"I know you were"—I searched for a word—"fond of her."

"If you want to know the truth," Harry said, "that's been wearing off for a while. It was kind of a relief when John showed up."

Hope is the thing with feathers. A little bird inside my chest began to stretch his wings.

"So," Harry said briskly. "How was the cruise?"

"Well," I began, but then he stopped me.

"Forget that I asked." He rubbed his forehead miserably. "I'm sure you and Tommy had a wonderful time."

"I guess you haven't been watching the news."

He looked at me. "What do you mean?"

"Does the name Dolores mean anything to you?"

"Is that his ex-wife?"

"Worse. A tropical storm."

Harry looked at me like a man who dares to hope. "There's a strange message from Amber on the machine. Something about the cruise getting rerouted, and she wanted us to call her as soon as we got home. I didn't pick up because I didn't want her to know I wasn't with you."

"The kids haven't found out, then?" I asked.

Harry shook his head. "I've been lying pretty low." Suddenly a big smile broke across his face. "So, there was a storm? And you had a terrible time?"

I filled him in. He was positively beaming. Then his smile faded.

"But of course," he said, "you still have another week off. I guess you and Tommy—"

"There is no me and Tommy. There *was* no me and Tommy. At least"—I tried not to smile, remembering Harry's own words—"nothing significant."

"So you kissed him?"

"Yes."

"But nothing else."

"Yes."

"And why should I believe you?"

His smile told me he already did.

"Because he's still dealing with Jessica," I said firmly. "And I'm in love with you."

"Really?" He spoke in a voice I could barely hear.

"Really."

For a moment, neither of us said anything.

"I screwed up, Francie."

"I screwed up, too."

"I started it."

"Okay," I said, smiling. "You can have full share of the blame if you want it."

"I need to ask you something, though," he said. "It's been bothering me for a while."

I took a deep breath. "Okay."

"Why didn't you tell me that you and Lucy went to high school together?"

This was the last thing I'd been expecting.

"It . . . didn't seem important," I finally said.

"But she stole your boyfriend, didn't she?" Harry said. "Arnie somebody."

I gaped at him. "She told you that?"

He nodded. "At our last meeting . . . well, I was pretty upset. I told everybody what I'd done and that you were gone and that I didn't think you'd ever forgive me. But Lucy said she thought you would. She said that, long ago, you'd forgiven her for something she had done. She said you had a forgiving heart."

For the first time, he looked at me. He took both my hands in his own.

"So tell me," he said, "is she right? Can you really forgive me?"

A forgiving heart. I have to say, I liked the sound of those words. I liked it that Lucy would think of me that way, particularly since it hadn't been true. And I liked the way Harry was rubbing his thumbs across my palms, the way he was pulling me toward him, the way he was taking me into his arms.

"Yes," I told Harry. "I forgive you."

"Happy anniversary," he said against my ear.

It was official. Harry and I had been married for twenty-five years.

*　　*　　*

I FORGAVE HARRY and Harry forgave me. The weight-loss study was extended and the rest of the summer passed quickly and happily. On the day of his "graduation," I was the first to shake Lucy's hand. Harry still wasn't thin, but he looked right for Harry. And by limiting his carbs to sixty a day, he was able to maintain his new weight.

In the fall, when Krys and John put their house on the market, I can't say that I wept. For his part, Harry didn't shed any tears when he learned that Tommy was taking a leave of absence. It turned out that Tommy had applied to a number of graduate programs in poetry. The two of us remained good—if cautious—friends until he left for New York, even though I knew he was less happy about my reconciliation with Harry than I would have been had he reconciled with Jessica. Not that there was much chance of that. No, I hoped he would meet somebody new. Perhaps another poet. Someone who could talk about *revisionists* and quote long, violent poems about flowers.

Harry's company, after several more delays, finally did have its IPO. There was a rather nice spike in the price of shares, and Harry sold 20 percent of our holdings immediately—the maximum amount permitted. This turned out to be an excellent call because within a few weeks the stock dropped well below its

original value. Still, we'd made enough to pay off our mort-
gage, and even after taxes, there was a little something left over.
Enough to repave the driveway. Enough to give each of the kids
a little gift. And enough to cover the cost of two more first-class
airline tickets to Miami.

The class-action lawsuit filed by the ship's two thousand
passengers had been settled quickly and quietly. Not that the
Czarina's legal eagles acknowledged any wrongdoing on the
part of the captain. Still, they were delighted to refund the price
of our original tickets, in addition to issuing new ones, out of
the simple goodness of their hearts. In September, Harry and I
boarded the *Czarina* for another one-week cruise, and if anyone—the children, our neighbors, even my mother—thought it
was strange that we'd repeat the same vacation so soon, none
of them broached the subject.

This time, the weather was perfect. We strolled the outer
decks, looking at the moon. We swam in the heated pools. We
took courses in couples massage, low-carb cooking, tai chi. We
made love in the king-sized bed. And we talked, and we talked,
and we talked. At last, things were back to normal. The past
few months didn't matter anymore. They were merely a series
of missteps easily retraced, the sort of mistakes any traveler
makes during the course of a lifelong journey.

On our last night aboard the *Czarina,* I awakened with the
sense that I was all alone. I sat up, switched on the light. A note
on Harry's pillow said, *Went for a walk,* and I realized that it
was the sound of him leaving that had awakened me. I got up
and pulled on shorts and a T-shirt. The ship was silent, the
ocean still. Where could he have gone? Restless, I wandered
about the room before settling into the love seat. I was hungry,

achingly hungry, but I didn't want anything to eat. Or at least I didn't want anything I might find aboard the *Czarina*. After nearly a week of grazing through endless low-carb buffets, and sitting down to five-course low-carb dinners, and snacking on low-carb confections, I had completely lost my appetite. I was tired of cheese and butter and cream, tired of lamb chops and swordfish and shrimp. Gladly would I have committed a felony for a simple cracker, a piece of toast, even a bite of a cinnamon roll.

"Last night I dreamed about bread again," I'd told Harry as we lay drowsing in a pool of starlight from the balcony.

"I know. You were grinding your teeth."

"If only I'd had the sense to pack some emergency Hostess cupcakes."

"You'd never have gotten them aboard. They have carb-sniffing beagles, you know, to check for contraband."

"They do not."

"If you're caught with more than thirty grams, they confiscate all your property."

I must have fallen asleep, because I opened my eyes to find Harry standing over me.

"Where—?" I began, but he put a finger to his lips.

"Put your shoes on," he whispered, "and come with me."

He took my hand and led me through the dark halls of the ship. When we reached the bank of elevators, instead of boarding one of the plush passenger cabs, Harry hustled me into the waiting service elevator.

"We're not supposed to use these," I said, pointing to the key pad. "Look, you need a special code."

"*Shh.*" To my amazement, Harry punched in some numbers, and the doors closed with a groan. The elevator descended down and down into the belly of the ship. We stepped out into a hall that clearly wasn't meant for passengers to see. The floors were bare gray concrete. A long flat hose stretched along one wall. There were fire extinguishers. Axes and gaffs. Warily, I eyed a coil of chains. Above us, the exposed pipes gleamed.

Again, Harry took my hand.

"Hurry," he said, breaking into a trot.

Rounding the corner, I nearly screamed at the sight of a steward. The steward looked as if he was about to scream himself. He wasn't much older than Jason, and in the dim, flickering light, his skin seemed oddly yellow. "Where have you been?" he hissed at Harry. His bared front teeth were a little too long, giving him the look of a nervous rat. "I could lose my job for this, you know."

Harry pulled out his wallet, peeled out a couple of bills. The steward snatched at them hastily.

"One hour," he squeaked. "Not one minute more."

He turned and, shielding his hands from Harry, punched another key pad mounted beside a narrow metal door. The door popped open. The steward glared at Harry one more time, then scurried away without looking back.

"Watch your step," Harry said, leading me over the high threshold.

Inside was a long, low-ceilinged room, divided by a single metal table. There were benches on either side, cluttered bulletin boards on the walls. A large graphic poster, spattered with grease, demonstrated the Heimlich maneuver.

"Where on earth are we?" I asked Harry.

"Staff cafeteria," he said. "What do you think?"

"Charming."

Harry grinned. "Have a seat. I've got a surprise for you."

He thumped the metal bench with his palm; it rang out like a gong. Then he disappeared through another door.

As soon as I heard the rattle of pots and pans, I understood. My heart sank. Harry was going to cook for me. Any other time, I would have thought it was romantic: sneaking into the kitchen to indulge on chilled lobster and caviar, a plate of rare sliced beef. But truly, all I wanted was a potato. A potato chip. A rice cake. And then—

I heard it before I smelled it.

Pop. Pop-pop.

Moments later, I could smell it, too—the thick, greasy, heavenly odor of popcorn popped in oil. I closed my eyes to better inhale the scent of the melting butter. I pricked my ears for the dry, crumbling sound it made as Harry shook it out of the pot. A few final *pops* of protest. The faint hiss of salt. He carried the bowl in like a wedding cake and placed it before me on the table. My mouth flooded with expectation. I reached out a trembling hand.

"There's plenty more where this came from," Harry said, sitting down beside me. "Other stuff, too. White bread. Doughnuts. Cornflakes. I figured they weren't feeding the staff surf and turf."

The first buttery kernel turned to velvet on my tongue. A little moan escaped my lips, and I looked at him with shining eyes.

"Good as you remember?" Harry asked, twining his foot around mine.

"God, yes." I grabbed another handful. "Don't you want any?"

"Maybe just a taste."

He caught my hand and nibbled a few kernels off the top. He wiped a grain of salt from my lips and slipped his finger into his mouth. I stared at him, amazed.

"How long has it been since you've had popcorn?" I asked.

He traced his finger beneath my lower lip. Kissed me.

"Quite a while."

"And you're happy with just a taste?"

He kissed me again, pulled me up, and eased me back on the table.

"Francie," he murmured into my hair. "Don't you know there's more to life than food?"

I had thought that things were back to normal. I was wrong.

They were better than ever.